W9-CIC-492

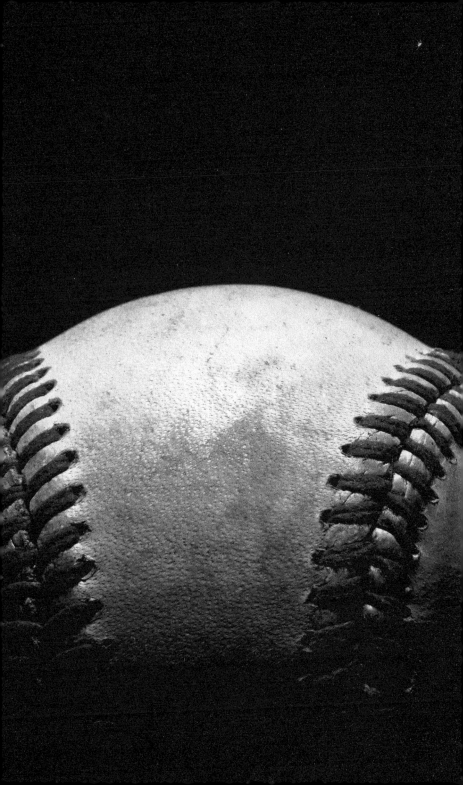

Also by Josh Berk

Strike Three, You're Dead

SAY IT AIN'T SO

LENNY & THE MIKES

JOSH BERK

ALFRED A. KNOPF

NEW YORK

THIS IS A BORZOI BOOK PUBLISHED BY ALFRED A. KNOPF

Visit us on the Web! randomhouse.com/kids

Educators and librarians, for a variety of teaching tools,
visit us at RHTeachersLibrarians.com

Library of Congress Cataloging-in-Publication Data
Berk, Josh.
Say it ain't so / by Josh Berk.
pages cm
"Lenny & the Mikes."
Summary: "Lenny gets jealous when Mike makes the school baseball team,
but together they and Other Mike stumble upon a stealing signals scandal that
could go further up than anyone knows"—Provided by publisher.
ISBN 978-0-375-87009-5 (hardcover) —
ISBN 978-0-375-97009-2 (library binding) —
ISBN 978-0-375-98737-3 (ebook)
[1. Baseball—Fiction. 2. Best friends—Fiction. 3. Friendship—Fiction.
4. Sports—Corrupt practices—Fiction. 5. Mystery and detective stories.]
I. Title.
PZ7.B452295Say 2014
[Fic]—dc23
2013015225

The text of this book is set in 12.5-point Goudy.

Printed in the United States of America

March 2014

10 9 8 7 6 5 4 3 2 1

First Edition

It looks like Schwenkfelder is going to the bullpen. By-ron Lucas contributed a solid outing, stepping in to start game one of the play-offs in place of Hunter Ashwell. Byron wasn't perfect, but he gave the Mustangs the lead. He gave the Mustangs the chance to win. That's all you can ever ask. But it looks like he's out of gas. Griffith's bats started to wake up last inning. They hit the ball hard and brought the game to a score of two to one. Schwenkfelder is ahead by one run. Here we are, getting ready to start the top of the seventh. The final inning.

The head coach confers with his assistant. And yes, they make the call to the bullpen. They're going to turn the ball over to— Oh my goodness, the call goes to the newest addition to the team. They call him "the Luna-tic," and from the looks of it, it's with good reason. He's a wild man out there on the mound. He has less control than a toddler in potty training. He's firing warm-up tosses like a blind monkey playing darts. Not a lot of strikes, but the coaches must have faith in him to put him into a high-pressure situation like this.

One more move on the field—the Lunatic's "personal catcher" comes in from first base and takes his customary spot behind the plate. He's the human backstop. The best catcher at stopping wild pitches the league has ever seen. Knowing he's there to block pitches has to give the Lunatic some confidence. But still, it's tense out there.

The game is on the line. The season is on the line. The championship trophy is on the line.

It's all, as they say, on the line.

The Lunatic nods his head. He's ready. He adjusts his cap and steps to the mound. The catcher flashes the sign and the Lunatic nods again. Here's the windup, and the pitch. . . .

CHAPTER ONE

I could tell it was going to be a good year when Mike called me up on New Year's Day and asked me to kick him in the crotch. I'm sorry—did I say "good year"? I meant "sorta-terrible-really-bad-then-kind-of-cool-but-mostly-just-weird year." I guess you could simply say it was going to be an interesting year.

Last year ended on a bad note, so I should have predicted weirdness. The holidays around the Norbeck house were just *awful*. My parents (mostly Mom) got it into their heads that we shouldn't celebrate Hanukkah *or* Christmas. My dad is Jewish and my mom is Christian, so usually we'd celebrate both. I was always pretty pleased with this arrangement, as you can imagine. It meant the old eight days of gifts during Hanukkah and still a pretty sweet Christmas haul. Presents galore! Trees *and* menorahs! Candy canes *and* potato pancakes! Actually, I don't really like potato pancakes. And candy canes always start out exciting but end up being disappointing. They're basically just a sticky mess you're sick of before you're even halfway done. But that's beside the point. The point is, every December for the first twelve years of my young life was awesome.

Not this one.

This year, Mom said, we'd still celebrate the *spirit* of those holidays, but when it came to gift getting, we'd celebrate zilch. I'm not kidding! *Zero! Zip! Nada!* She had it in her head that I had way too many toys and things. So her brilliant idea was that instead of Christmas or Hanukkah, we'd celebrate *Discardia*. Yeah, I had never heard of it either. It's a made-up holiday. And okay, maybe all the holidays are made-up holidays if you think about it. Ever look at one of those calendars that has every holiday on it? There are some weird ones. Grandparents Day? Administrative Professionals Week? National Mustard Day? (That's actually a pretty good one that I look forward to every year.)

But seriously, sports fans, I would have *much* preferred celebrating Principals Day for a whole month to the travesty that is Discardia. . . . (Yeah,

Principals Day is also a real one. I wonder who made *that* up. . . .)

Picture me waking up on the morning of December 25. The room is *not* packed to the gills with presents. There are no stockings hung by the chimney with care. There are no halls decked with boughs of holly. No fa! No la! No la-la-la-la-la-la-la! Instead, by the tree there is an empty wheelbarrow. This would be bad enough if the wheelbarrow were your only gift. (Unless you were some sort of barrow collector and the wheelbarrow was the last one you needed for your barrow collection.) But no, not in the Norbeck house. During Discardia the wheelbarrow is there to *steal* your toys. To cart away your happiness like some sort of Grinch on wheels. (Grinch on *wheel*, I guess.)

On the morning of Discardia you glumly fill up this wheelbarrow with your favorite toys. Okay, at first it's not your *favorites*. At first it's the oldest and worst toys you're not even sure why you still own. It's the broken trucks, the outdated video games, the superhero action figures missing one or both legs. A puzzle of the Rocky Mountains you lost, like, ninety pieces to and you never really liked doing anyway. Books you are more than glad to get out of reading. But no, these things will not make your mother happy. She will invite you to "dig deeper." To "truly give." To "give until it hurts." You respond that it already hurts, even though you should know better than to say anything. Because any time you say anything, Mom just launches into another speech.

"Lenny, don't you know that others have nothing? Nothing at all! Others would be happy with just a warm meal. Others would be thrilled just to have a roof over their heads. Others would *appreciate* things."

"Hey," you say. "If others are so easy to please, then they're sure going to love this Spider-Man head! I have no idea where the body is."

When will you learn? Why do you say things like this? Because the response is just more speeches.

"Lenny, I am truly disappointed in you. You have a chance to make yourself a better person this Christmas season. Isn't that the greatest gift of all? You have the chance to make yourself a better person *and* the chance to brighten the life of some poor kid who has nothing, and you're going to make jokes? You're going to throw a fit that you don't have the new baseball game for the video-game machine?"

You want to point out that you already do have

the new baseball game and that no one says "video-game machine," but by now you've learned your lesson. You want to point to the new car in the driveway and ask Mom when she plans on giving that away. You want to point to the jewelry around her neck and the rings on her fingers. But you don't. You know that saying this would be a terrible idea. You know that saying this would probably make said baseball game end up in the wheelbarrow. So you shut your mouth and bite your tongue.

You give till it hurts.

Then you give some more.

CHAPTER TWO

By the end of the holiday break I was pretty bummed and (gasp!) feeling ready to go back to school. It was awful hanging around the house, thinking about everyone else's presents. Pennsylvania winters are cold and wet and icy. All of December had been mostly just slush—not even a snowfall decent enough to chuck snowballs or bust out the sled.

Too wet to go out, and too cold to play ball. That's me quoting Dr. Seuss. Shut up, I know it's a baby book, but it's stuck in my head because Dad used to read it to me nine million times. I still have my copy with a homemade bookplate reading LENNY'S FAVORITE BOOK pasted inside. Only, *favorite* is spelled wrong. Come to think of it, so is *book*. And let's be honest, the odds are beyond pretty good that I put five extra Ns in *Lenny's* and made the *E* backward. LƎNNNNNNNY'S FAVRETE BOK. Whatever. I was, like, four.

Also, every year around the first of January I start to get jittery from not having baseball to watch. This year was especially rough since the Phillies flamed out in the first round of the playoffs. The off-season was long and cold and as black as a starless night.

I will say that seventh grade at Schwenkfelder Middle School was shaping up to be quite a bit nicer than sixth. Me and my best friends (Mike and Other Mike) were sort of legends of the seventh grade. I mean, not everyone cared, but we did get somewhat famous the previous summer. How? Oh, only by solving the biggest crime in Philadelphia Phillies history. Part of the chase for a murderer (which eventually led us into the line of fire and also the Phillies dugout) introduced to us our favorite player, catcher Ramon Famosa. Of course, that turned out not to be his real name. And when I say "our favorite player," I mainly mean me and Mike. Other Mike has no interest in baseball. He's mainly into books about wizards—sorry, warlocks. There is an important distinction that escapes me, but Other Mike would be really happy to tell you all about it and probably make a presentation that would last a few hours.

The point is that something kinda major happened when we met Ramon Famosa, something besides almost getting killed in a shopping mall. Famosa saw Mike grab a video camera out of the air and block a sprinting little person from stealing it. It was a pretty awesome move by Mike, I thought. Famosa agreed. He told Mike that he should be a catcher. Now, when a big-league catcher tells you that you have the right stuff to be a catcher yourself, you're going to think about it. Ramon Famosa telling you that you could be a catcher is like Leonardo da Vinci telling you to go pick up a paintbrush. Which would be really impressive on account of da Vinci being dead. But I can't think of any painter who is alive, so just go with me here. The only problem with that whole idea is that there's a reason Mike quit baseball. His arm. Mike was a pretty good pitcher when we were about nine. That was the same year that I quit due to a highly embarrassing reason that I don't want to mention again if I don't have to. But Mike quit due to his arm injury.

Mike is sort of a stubborn personality, so he

didn't listen to any of the repeated warnings from his coaches about resting his arm. He'd pitch the maximum number of pitches allowed in Little League and then go home and throw a million more fast ones into the pitching screen in the backyard. His shoulder got pretty bad and he had to take a break from pitching. He could have played a different position and stayed on the team, but like I said, Mike is pretty stubborn. He had it in his mind that he'd be a pitcher or nothing, and so nothing it was.

Let me say that part of me thought that maybe he was also quitting baseball to be a good friend to me. My career was *definitely* over, so maybe he was quitting out of solidarity? Yeah, right.

CHAPTER THREE

On New Year's Day, as I left our house and rode my bike to Mike's house, it had (finally!) just started to snow. Not enough to stick to the ground and extend winter vacation, which would have ruled, but enough to dust the grass and stick in everyone's hair. The flakes landed like dandruff in my black hair as I finished the short ride, parked my bike in the driveway, and rang the doorbell at Mike's house.

Mike's mom answered the door. She was carrying a basket of laundry on her hip. "How many times have I told you that you don't have to ring the doorbell?" she asked. "You're like family."

"Thanks," I said. "I always forget. The cardiologists trained me to be polite, I guess."

"It's weird that you call your parents 'the cardiologists,'" she said as I came in the front door and took off my boots. I just shrugged.

"Mike around?" I asked. It was a dumb question because I knew that he was.

"Garage," she said. "It's freezing, but he's been out there all morning hitting off the tee." I heard a *thwack* of bat against ball as if to prove her point.

"I guess now he wants to work on his defense," I said.

"Don't tell me that you're here to help him test out his cup," she said.

"Ha-ha," I said. "Yeah. How did you know?"

"He asked me to kick him in the crotch this morning. I told him there are just some limits to a mother's love. His sister volunteered, but I thought that wasn't the best idea."

"Yeah, there's a pretty good chance that would have ended badly," I agreed.

The *thwack* sounds from the garage stopped, and a second later Mike walked into the foyer. It might have been an optical illusion, but he seemed bigger than the last time I saw him, which was just the other day. He was filling up almost the whole doorway. He was sweating despite the cold and breathing a little heavily.

"Hey, Len," he said. "You might want to look into using that bottle of Head & Shoulders I gave you for Hanukkah."

"Huh?" I said.

"Your hair." He pointed with the batter's glove on his left hand. "Snow makes it look like you got dandruff."

"Oh yeah," I said. "I was just thinking that." I took off my coat and hung it on the rack by the door. Mike's house always had a great smell and a lot of snacks. It was hard not to be in a good mood when you walked in the door, no matter how bizarre a mission you were on.

"Weird thing is, I *wish* I would have gotten a bottle of dandruff shampoo for Hanukkah," I said. "Better than nothing."

"Better than having to *give away* stuff," he said. "I still can't believe that."

"Yeah, but, you know, it's making me a better person and all that."

"Do you *feel* like a better person?"

"Oh yeah," I said. "I feel like the greatest person in the world. I feel like if Martin Luther King Jr. and Mother Teresa had a baby."

"But you'd trade it all to get your video games back?"

"Ha-ha, yeah. Trade it in a heartbeat."

"Mother Teresa would be proud," he said. "Listen, I have to go get the cup. You head into the garage. I'll meet you in there in a sec."

I headed into the garage. It was packed to the gills with empty boxes that had held the toys Mike and his little sister, Arianna, had gotten for Christmas. I tried not to be jealous. There was also a spot in the garage where Mike had cleared away the boxes, garbage cans, old shoes, and other random junk that always fills everyone's garages. He had turned this area into his little catcher-training gym. He apparently was taking it very seriously. There was a catcher's mitt, of course, and some balls, as well as dumbbells and even a book from the library on how to be a catcher.

It was a really old book. Maybe it was the only book they had in at the time, or maybe Mike's dad was remembering it from his childhood and checked it out. Johnny Bench was on the cover, and the title was *Hey, You! Be a Better Ballplayer! Become a Star Catcher!* Apparently, *Be a Better Ballplayer!* was a whole series. Also, apparently, the author really! liked! exclamation! points! The 1970s were a pretty exciting time, I guess. Sideburns!

Mike was taking a long time getting his cup on. I suppose it's a pretty delicate procedure. I've never worn one myself and don't fancy that I ever will, thank you very much. I skimmed most of *Hey, You! Be a Better Ballplayer! Become a Star Catcher!* and it was not really worthy of such exciting punctuation, I can tell you that. It had lots of the basics about how to crouch and call pitches. A riveting chapter on footwork. A bunch about how to throw. We can only assume that Mike skipped over the throwing sections and just hoped somehow that wouldn't be a major part of his game. I guess he could throw out a runner if he had to—it was the repetitive stress of pitching that was messing up his shoulder.

There were also lots of old-school tips on "getting tough." This was apparently a big part of being a catcher. You were supposed to spend a lot of time punching your catching hand with your other hand. I guess the idea was that it would numb the nerves or build up calluses or something. I tried it, but felt silly. It looked like I was itching to start a fight with someone.

Finally Mike came back into the garage. I knew he was wearing a cup but I tried not to look down there. This was getting weird.

"Um, ready?" I asked.

"As I'll ever be," he said. "If I'm going to make

the team, I'm going to have to get used to this. You know, Davis Gannett has no fear of the fastball."

"Davis Gannett has no fear of anything," I said. Davis was an eighth grader and the current starting catcher on the Schwenkfelder Middle School baseball team. He was as big as a high school senior and it wouldn't have surprised me to find out that he was actually twenty-five. The kind of kid who might have flunked a few grades—say, ten or fifteen. He had a little mustache and a shaved head. Most of the kids at Schwenkfelder had this blow-dried side-combed haircut like a certain pop star made popular. Not Davis Gannett. He had a head shaved so close it must have been done with a straight razor. What hair he did have was very light, blond to the point of being almost white. It made him look like an old man. It made him look like a serial killer.

Mike took a deep breath, closed his eyes, and said, "Let 'er rip."

I brought back my right foot and did as I was told. I kicked Mike in the crotch. Hard.

He didn't even blink. "Is that all you got?" he said. He yawned and cracked his knuckles.

"Just warming up," I said. I took a step back and really let him have it. Again, not even a blink. It was then that I knew he was going to make the team. He was going to be a star. It was also then that Mike's little sister, Arianna, walked into the garage. She had grown a lot in the past year. She was, much to my annoyance, like, almost as tall as me. She was terrifying as a tiny person, so now she was, well, whatever is beyond terrifying. She always hated me for some reason, and the feeling was beginning to be mutual.

"My turn! My turn!" she said.

"No way," Mike said. "Get out of here. I don't want you anywhere near me, Arianna."

"I don't want to kick *you*," she said. "I want to kick Lenny."

"I'm not even wearing a cup!" I said.

"I know," she said, narrowing her eyes. "That's my point."

Mike and I looked at each other. He started to laugh. I did not.

"Uh, can we go do something else?" I asked.

"You go ahead inside," he said. "I have a few more drills I need to practice. You can check out my new toys." Then he paused for a second and hastily added, "Sorry."

"No need to apologize to me," I said. "You didn't invent Discardia."

"Oooh," he said. "Actually, I did. I'm also behind National Mustard Day. And Have a Bad Day Day."

I should have laughed. It *was* a pretty good one. But I was feeling so glum. It wasn't just the toys. It wasn't just that Mike was obviously going to make the team while I sat on the sidelines. It was more than that. He had this . . . this thing he was so excited to do. Little League is big around here, yeah, but the middle school baseball team is what's really huge. Mainly because the high school baseball team is always great. It's a pretty small school, but they had an amazing history of success.

Schwenkfelder High's baseball team (Fighting Quakers!) wins the division pretty much every year. They won the state championship in 1982 and I think that was the biggest thing to ever happen to Schwenkfelder. I don't just mean the high school—I mean the whole town. There is still a giant blue and white banner hanging over the front door of the high school: SCHWENKFELDER HIGH SCHOOL—PENNSYLVANIA STATE BASEBALL CHAMPIONS 1982. The only other banner is the one that says ADEQUATE YEARLY ACADEMIC SCORES! You can tell that they're way more excited about the baseball. Actually, it's really funny that they even made a banner celebrating being adequate. Maybe some-one complained that they should celebrate academic stuff as much as sports, but the best thing they could say about the school's academics was "adequate." That exclamation point isn't fooling anyone.

The guys who played on that 1982 team are still kind of legends around town. The current head coach was one of those guys—one of the pitchers from that '82 team. His name is Gary Hinzo and everyone calls him "Coach Zo." Short for "Hinzo," I guess. The assistant coach—Ray Moyer—was on that team too.

Another local legend was Pete Benderson, who everyone calls "Bendy." Baseball nicknames aren't really that inventive a lot of the time. I mean, yeah, sometimes there's "Old Tomato Face" (Gabby Hartnett) or "Puddin' Head" (Willie Jones). Usually it's like, "Hey, let's call Willie McCovey just 'Mac.' Christy Mathewson? Let's call him 'Matty.' Mike Lieberthal? 'Lieby.'" Basically, you just take the first syllable of their last name and maybe add a y. . . . I guess I'd be "Norb"? Or maybe "Norby"? Doesn't sound that cool. Maybe I'd get a good one. I would do anything for a great nickname. Wouldn't really want to be "Old Tomato Face," though. Possibly I could be like Garry Maddox: "the Secretary of Defense." Do you think people really called him that, though? Like out at dinner? "Hey, the Secretary of Defense, could you pass the pepper?" Probably they just called him "Garry."

Anyway, Bendy was the star center fielder of 1982 and supposedly got a tryout with the Phils. He didn't make it, but he was still a big shot and the most popular barber in town despite giving truly awful haircuts. Dads just wanted to take their kids there to hear his baseball stories of years ago.

My point is, any kid on the high school team pretty much had it made. So the excitement started young. T-ball could get intense. Making the middle school team was like getting signed to the minors— the first step on a journey to the big time. You could have ugly clothes and your haircut could be the old Benderson special—long in front and short in random spots—but if you were on the baseball team, you'd be a golden child.

So Mike had this ahead of him. State championships. Trophies. His name on a plaque. Everybody looking up to him. A half-decent career as a barber. What did I have to look forward to? Last year was pretty cool—winning that contest and solving the mystery of Blaze O'Farrell. But what was next? Had I already had my one and only moment in the sun? Were the clouds already gathering on the life of Lenny Norbeck?

"Ah, I'm just gonna head home," I said. "I'm not feeling so great." It wasn't the truth but it wasn't exactly a lie.

"Oh, okay," Mike said with a shrug. "I guess I'll see you at school on Monday."

"Yeah," I said. "Sure thing."

Before I even finished the short sentence, Mike was back with his nose in *Hey, You! Be a Better Ballplayer! Become a Star Catcher!* He was muttering under his breath, "The positioning of a catcher's feet is of utmost importance." Practicing his footwork, I guess. I heard his sneakers squeaking on the garage floor as I turned to ride home.

CHAPTER FOUR

Back at school on a cold Monday morning, the talk through the halls was all of gifts received.

"You got the new first-person shooter game *War-Face 5: Faces of War-Face*?! Yeah, me too!"

"You got a bike? Awesome!"

"Yeah, but it's too cold to ride it."

"So what? Bike's always a great gift."

I just listened. I had nothing to add. You know what's *not* a great gift? Giving away all your stuff. So, yeah, I kept my head down and my mouth shut. At lunch it was pretty much the same.

I tried to be friendly as the Mikes discussed their haul. Other Mike was going on and on about the new *Warlock Wallop* boxed set he got. Twenty-two books.

"Don't you already own all twenty-two?" Mike asked.

"Sure," Other Mike said, talking louder than necessary. It was noisy in the cafeteria, but he was, like, yelling. "But this set includes newly drawn maps and character bio sheets and the box itself! Oh man, it's made out of real dragon leather. Well, okay, not real dragon leather, but it feels just like it!"

I wanted to ask Other Mike how he (or anyone) knows what real dragon leather feels like. And also how you could even make leather out of dragons anyway. Weren't they covered in scales? But I wasn't feeling nearly chipper enough for this sort of conversation. I just nodded my head up a little as if to say "Oh yeah," and went back to eating my turkey sandwich. It tasted kind of gross and I chewed without enjoyment.

Mike listened patiently and then proceeded to tell Other Mike about *his* Christmas gifts. It was of course all catching gear. Catcher's mask, chest protector, shin guards, training DVDs, and whatever else. Probably a diamond-encrusted cup. Other Mike didn't know all that much about baseball, but he did know that Mike used to be a pitcher and quit after his injury. Specifically, Mike had said: "If I can't pitch, I don't play. It's the most important part of the game and the only part I want to do."

When Other Mike quoted this back at Mike now, Mike launched into a speech. It almost sounded like he'd been practicing it.

"You know—I've been thinking about it. Catchers get no credit. It's not fair. They're actually the most important player on the team."

Other Mike only shrugged as if to agree. But I couldn't let this go. I simply couldn't. It was Mike himself who always said the pitcher was most important. And now, just because catching was his new kick, he thought it was the most important thing in the world? Just because a catcher saw him tackle a guy in a shopping mall meant that Mike was the best catcher ever?

"Well, I don't know if I'd say *most* important," I said, swallowing the slimy mass of turkey.

"What, pitcher?" Mike asked.

"Well, kind of. The catcher wouldn't have a lot to do without a pitcher. He'd just be a guy squatting in the dirt looking like he's trying to take a poop on the side of the road."

Other Mike laughed and coughed on his milk. I smiled a little. Mike did *not* smile. He chomped angrily on a potato chip.

"The catcher *makes* the pitcher," he said. "A good catcher can make a bad pitcher good and a good pitcher great. It's our job to instill confidence. To call a good game."

"If you say so," I said. I wiped my mouth. I was trying to stay calm but I could feel my heart start to beat faster.

"What?" Mike said.

"I said, 'If you say so.' What?"

"You're disagreeing with me."

"I am not," I said. Though, yeah, I kind of was. I felt myself getting angrier.

"Are too!"

"Now you're disagreeing with me about whether or not I'm disagreeing with you."

Other Mike laughed again, but this time it was a nervous sort of laugh. Kind of like a hiccup. Like a *huh-whuh* more than a *ha-ha*.

"Is something bothering you, Lenny?" Mike asked, his voice getting louder. "You've been acting weird for a long time."

"Oh, I've been acting weird? You spend all your time punching yourself and asking people to kick you in the crotch, and *I'm* acting weird?"

"Let it out, Lenny. Let it all out. You're jealous of me and you know it."

"I am not! I'm happy for you. Or at least I was. Until you got so freaking high and mighty on your horse. Catchers aren't the most important thing in the world. They just catch the ball. Just because you are one now. Funny how that works. How whatever you are happens to be the most important thing in the world."

I guess my voice must have been getting really loud at this point because all the tables around us got a little quiet. I felt a bunch of eyeballs staring at me. I felt my ears burn hot and my blood run cold. Then I heard a voice.

"Hey, what are you dork-buckets arguing about?" the voice asked us. "Trying to figure out which one of you is a bigger dork-bucket? I got the answer for you: it's a three-way tie for first place. All three of you are coholders of the world's largest dork-bucket trophy. There, I solved the mystery for you. Now please stop yelling so I can go back to enjoying my three lunches."

The voice belonged to Davis Gannett, just about the worst person a voice could belong to. As I mentioned before, he was a mean-looking eighth grader who towered over everyone with his shaved head and fierce gaze. Other things to know about Davis Gannett: He liked to call everyone dork-buckets (obviously) and thought he was hilarious. Also, he was the catcher on the Schwenkfelder

Middle School baseball team. Everyone knew this. Everyone except Other Mike.

Other Mike also did not know when it was a good time to keep your mouth shut. Times like, say, when a mean teacher is serious about giving the class detention for one more peep. Times like, say, when a bad guy with a gun is telling you to be quiet. Times like when Davis Gannett was standing at your lunch table calling you a dork-bucket.

"No," Other Mike said, blissfully ignorant. "We were actually arguing about which is a more important position in baseball—pitcher or catcher. I have no opinion on the matter personally, but Lenny here is defending the pitcher, while Other Mike is all about being a catcher."

"Is that right, dork-bucket?" Davis said, addressing Mike directly. He spoke in a low, quiet voice. It was almost a growl. He sounded like a grizzly bear. A grizzly bear who has been smoking a few hundred cigarettes every day for a few decades. "You're all about being a catcher? As in you just want to join my fan club? Tell me it's not that you want my job on the team?"

"Oh, Davis, are you a catcher too?" Other Mike said.

"What do you mean *too*?" Davis snarled.

"Um, as in 'also'?" Other Mike offered, not very helpfully. "I know it's confusing because it can also mean the preposition *to* or the number *two*." As always, the point when a normal person would stop talking sailed right past and Other Mike continued to yammer. "Ha-ha," he said. "Number two. *That's* confusing because it can mean you're counting or it can also mean poop. Which reminds me of a funny thing Lenny just said earlier, which is that a catcher actually *looks* like he's taking a poop. What was it, Lenny? A catcher looks like someone squatting on the side of the road to take a poop?"

Davis just stood there, blinking, not quite able to believe any of this. I couldn't believe it either. What was Other Mike doing? Davis just kept blinking, staring, rubbing one of his huge hands over his sheared scalp.

"How about I take a poop in your milk, Lenny?" he said to me finally. He stared at me, not blinking. I guess he was actually waiting for an answer.

"No, well, I wouldn't like that really," I said. Honesty is the best policy! I sort of wanted to change the subject. To get it off of how I was making fun of catchers and to get it back to how Mike *was* trying to take Davis's spot on the team. But even though I was mad at Mike, I didn't exactly want to get him killed. Then Mike spoke up. He also stood up. His chair squeaked on the floor and somehow the cafeteria got even quieter. A chair squeaked in anger was a clear sign to shush. Was there really going to be a fight?

"Yeah, Davis," Mike said, his voice only shaking a little bit. "I'm a catcher too. I'm going to practice all winter long and come springtime I'll see you behind the plate. May the best man win, and please leave my friends alone." He thrust out his hand for Davis to shake it. Davis stared at it for a long moment, then slapped it away.

"Ha," he spat. "A dork-bucket like you taking *my* spot on the team? You think you know baseball now? Playing the game is a lot different than watching it on the couch—believe me." His voice climbed from a growl to a yell. "You dork-buckets think you're so great because you solved some mystery? Well, the only mystery you'll be solving is the case of the disappearing dork-buckets. And you know where they'll find you? Buried in a hole in the ground behind the dugout! Bring it, DiNuzzio. You're going down."

He grabbed the milk off my tray. For a brief, disturbing second I thought he was going to take a poop in it. Instead, he just chugged it in one big gulp, then threw the carton onto the ground.

Mr. Donovan, the hefty social studies teacher, came jogging (more like waddling, AM I RIGHT??) over, presumably to see what the fuss was about. Or maybe to tell Davis to pick up the milk carton. Davis ignored him, and made a rude gesture with his hand and stormed toward the exit. Mr. Donovan looked shocked. He slowly bent over to pick up the milk himself and followed Davis toward the door. Mr. Donovan moved so slowly Davis would probably be in Ohio by the time he caught up to him. The rest of us sat in silence.

I expected Other Mike to say something stupid, like how it would be sort of impossible for us to *solve* the mystery of the disappearing dork-buckets if we ourselves were the ones dead and buried. Which actually *wouldn't* have been a stupid thing to say, but rather a valid point. Anyway, Other Mike thankfully let it go. The bell rang. Lunch was over. Davis was off somewhere, probably pooping in milk cartons and/or getting detention again.

"Thanks, Mike," I said in a whisper. And I meant it.

CHAPTER FIVE

From that day forward, I knew what I had to do. I knew I had to help Mike make the team. What kind of friend would I be if I didn't at least do that? Soon the ground began to thaw and the birds started to return to their springtime squawking. Phils preseason games were visible on TV, shooting up like sprouts in the cold ground.

And then Mike's dad did something awesome: he built a pitcher's mound and backstop in the backyard. He got some dirt from wherever you buy dirt from. (Note: My fallback career from baseball announcer could be dirt salesman. Seems pretty easy. Dirt is everywhere. You just walk around picking it up in the woods and then put it in a bag to sell to people in the suburbs. Genius.)

Mr. Mike was pretty great at that kind of thing. One time when we were little he built an ice-skating rink in the front yard. And of course he invented the lawn couch. Heck of a guy. But he really outdid himself with the pitcher's mound. There was even a backstop and a real home plate fifty feet away. It was everything a budding catcher needed to learn to ply his trade. The only thing missing was someone to pitch to him.

Now, I mentioned before that I was not exactly a great baseball player. As a hitter, I was the type of kid who considered it a success if I managed a foul tip even when the coach pitched. You could tell he was trying really hard to hit my bat with his ball, but somehow the ball always jumped over my bat like a fly avoiding a fly swatter.

In T-ball, I usually just hit the tee and in fact broke enough tees and delayed enough games that I was nicknamed "the Human Rain Delay" (my first of many bad nicknames). This got me briefly banned from a kindergarten league. Kind of impressive, sure. But once we moved up to actually hitting live pitching was when my true stinkiness really started to shine. I went entire seasons without managing so much as a foul tip. The greatest day of my life was when I was hit by a pitch and got to experience the vast beauty of first base.

First base was so wonderful. So big. So white.

So soft. Like a velvety pillow. I wanted to lie down right there on it and fall asleep. Of course what you're supposed to do when you're on first base is run to second, especially if someone hits the ball. But there I was, lost in my beautiful joy of standing on first. The next batter was a girl named Martha Spearman, who actually was a good hitter. She laced the first pitch into right-center. I didn't notice and was immediately thrown out on a very rare putout from center field. Score it eight to four. Fielder's choice. Martha Spearman was sort of obsessed with her batting average and was furious that I had cost her a hit. And I was pretty sad my time on the base paths was over. I never returned.

So if you love baseball and stink at hitting, it makes sense to try to become a pitcher, right? That's what I thought. But somehow I was even worse at pitching than I was at hitting, if you can believe that. I read lots of tips on how to throw. I studied the moves of all my favorite pitchers. I got lessons from coaches and parents and friends. I'd take my spot on the mound, wind up, and fire what I was sure was going to be a strike right down the middle. Nope. Each time I let loose a pitch, the ball would take on a life of its own. It would bounce ten feet in front of the plate. It would sail over the backstop. On occasion, yes, the ball would fly backward out of my hand and land somewhere near center field or perhaps South Jersey. My dreams of being a star pitcher were pretty much dashed before I logged an inning.

So you can imagine that I was pretty skeptical when Mike called me up one Saturday to tell me about *my* role with the pitcher's mound.

"Dude, Len, you'll never believe what my dad did," he said.

"Oh, I'll believe it," I said. I don't know why I said that.

"He built a pitcher's mound in the backyard!"

"Awesome!" I said.

"Yeah," he said. "It's just the thing I need to practice my catching."

"Well, it's not *just* the thing," I said. "Unless he also built a pitching machine."

"That's where you come in," he said.

"I—I don't know how to build a pitching machine," I said. "Remember when we were supposed to build a car out of a mousetrap and I came in last place?"

"You also almost killed Mr. Thurston when the car exploded and shot a screw at his head."

"Good old Thirsty Thurston," I said. "I'm glad I didn't kill him."

"So listen, Len, I don't need you to build a pitching machine. I need you to *be* a pitching machine."

I saw where he was going with this. "Um, I think we know the only thing I'm worse at than building cars from mousetraps is pitching."

"Exactly why you're the man for the job, Norbeck. Remember when you almost killed Mr. Antonucci in gym class? He wasn't anywhere near home plate and your pitch knocked off his hat," Mike said.

"Man, I sure have almost killed teachers a lot of times. I'm, like, a stone-cold criminal. I don't know why you'd want to be my friend."

"Like I said, Lenny," he shot back. "You're just the man for the job."

"I don't get it. You want me to pitch to you *because* I stink at pitching?"

"Well, I didn't say you stink. . . ."

"Let's not beat around the bush, Mike," I said. "I seriously hate it whenever people beat around the bush. I'm, like, totally anti-bush-beating-around."

"Well, see, here's what I'm thinking: I'm never

going to be great at throwing guys out because I have this stupid weak shoulder. My game is going to have to be mostly about blocking pitches. I have to be the best at handling pitchers, stopping wild pitches, smothering anything that comes near me. That's the only weakness Davis Gannett has."

"You mean besides the fact that he's a terrible human being?" I said.

"Well, yes, there is also that," he said. "So will you do it?"

"You just want me to come over there and throw terrible pitches all over the place off the mound so you can practice blocking wild pitches?"

"You got it."

"You want not just a pitching machine, but a lean, mean, *wild*-pitching machine?"

"Yes."

"Say it."

"Leonard Norbeck, it would be my honor to request your presence at this pitcher's mound tomorrow. The pitcher's mound in my backyard that my dad built needs you. Because you are the world's greatest lean, mean, wild-pitching machine."

"I'm in, Mike," I said. "I'm in."

CHAPTER SIX

Sunday morning I got up bright and early. I found my baseball glove. It was easy to find. I had nailed it to the wall. Even though I don't really use it anymore, I convinced Mom to spare it from the carnage of Discardia. Things that didn't make it through the carnage: Pokémon cards, a telescope, some video games, and a set of juggling balls. I never learned how to juggle, but I really missed that stuff. Well, not really the telescope, which I hadn't used since I was about seven and briefly considered a career as an astronaut. Or astronomer? Astrologer? Something with *astro*—and not the Houston Astros. Anyway, I kept the glove just for, you know, sentimental reasons. That wasn't enough for Mom, so I took a nail and hung it on my wall and called it art. Getting it off was a pain, but finally I was ready.

Dad stuck his head in my room while I was pulling the glove off the wall.

"I thought that was your art?" he said.

"Yeah, well, surprisingly I need it to actually play baseball with."

"Good thing Mom didn't throw it away," he said. I was starting to guess that Dad wasn't the biggest Discardia fan in the world either. "I should have told her my golf clubs were art too, nailed them to the ceiling."

"Yeah," I said.

"So what inspired the need for the baseball glove?" he asked. "I thought you retired from the game."

"Yeah, well, sometimes the world needs a wild pitcher, and I'm the wildest pitcher that ever pitched a wild . . . pitch."

He looked a little confused. Like a man biting into a soft pretzel and finding it unexpectedly filled with cottage cheese.

"Going out for the team?" he asked. "Gonna be the secret weapon that helps the Mustangs win it all?"

"Nah," I laughed. "Just helping Mike. He's going to try out for catcher. I'm going to throw him some balls in the dirt, help him practice."

"Cool," he said. "Have fun. And, hey—if you see Mr. Mike, tell him I guess I'm out for golfing this spring." He sighed and shook his head glumly.

"Discardia sucks," I said.

Dad didn't say anything. He was honoring that unwritten rule that parents have to always stick together. But I could tell he agreed with me by the way he narrowed his eyes and rubbed his hand over his bald head. He walked down the hall staring at the ground. He looked like a toddler on the way to the naughty chair. Oh yeah, he agreed.

I got my bike out of the garage and headed over to Mike's house. This time I was not going to kick him in the crotch. This time I was going to throw wild pitches at him. The things we do for our friends. . . . It was kind of a chilly March day, the sky gray and hard. I rode quickly, pumping my legs, trying to get warm.

When I got there, Mike was already in full catcher's gear. He was standing in the driveway. He was doing that thing, banging his hands together to make them tough. It was weird, but at least he wasn't kicking himself in the crotch.

"Hey, Mike," I said. He lifted the catcher's mask. He looked pretty natural with that mask on, I had to admit.

"Hey, Len," he said. He spit on the driveway. "Come check out the mound."

I dropped my bike in the grass and followed him to the backyard. The pitcher's mound was truly an impressive sight. It looked just like someone dug up a real baseball stadium and dropped it into suburbia. There was even a backstop, which was probably going to come in handy. There was no way Mike could catch my pitches.

"Ain't nothing to it but to do it," Mike said. He slapped me on the rear end. He was taking this new persona as a catcher a little too far. Catchers were always doing that, slapping their pitcher on the tush.

Mike's dad had bought a whole bucket of balls, which Mike placed next to the mound. I picked one up, toed the rubber, and waited for Mike to take his crouch. It felt cool and I really wished that I was a *good* pitcher. It wasn't that fun to be asked as a freak. A wild-pitch specialist. Eh, what else was I going to do with my Sunday? Mom got rid of all my toys anyway.

"Are you going to give me signs or . . . ?" I asked, shouting to Mike from the mound.

He yelled through the mask. "Do you have a lot of pitches I should know about?"

"Just the high cheese, the high cheese, and the high cheese," I said. Calling a fastball the "high cheese" is, like, the funniest thing ever.

"Then bring the high cheese," he said.

I started my windup, announcing the whole time in my head. *Now entering the game is number thirty-three for the Philadelphia Phillies: Lenny Norbeck! Norbeck is known for his searing high cheese, of course, as well as leading the league in wild pitches by a wide margin. Here's the windup, and the pitch!*

I uncorked a heater so wild that Mike didn't even have a chance. I'm pretty sure Ramon Famosa, or any major-league catcher, wouldn't have had a chance. Pretty sure Plastic Man wouldn't have been able to snag it, and I don't know if you know this about him, but his arms are made out of plastic. It bounced about one-third of the way to home plate and came to a stop somewhere between the neighbor's yard and western Antarctica.

"Just getting warmed up," I said. "Keeping you on your toes."

Mike nodded his head and adjusted his mask. I grabbed another ball. I concentrated less on throwing it hard and more on just getting it near Mike. I took a deep breath and let it fly. It still hit the dirt, but only a few feet in front of the dish. Mike dropped from his crouch to his knees, and smothered the ball with his shin guards.

"Nice one!" I said.

He just nodded that helmet again and threw the ball back to me. I missed it, of course, and not only because my glove had a nail hole in it. But it didn't matter. I had a whole bucket of balls. I picked up another and another and another. We did this for what seemed like hours. Pitch by pitch. Some were so high Mike had to jump like a basketball player leaping for a rebound. Some so low they kicked up tornadoes of dirt at his feet. Many flew past Mike altogether and slapped into the backstop with a thud. A few joined their friend in the neighbor's yard. I really was the master of the wild pitch. But, hey, one or two even hit his glove. What's the expression? Even a blind squirrel finds a nut some days. I really was about as good a pitcher as a blind squirrel would be. But as the day went on and my arm grew sore, it was clear Mike was going to be a pretty good catcher. A *great* catcher.

CHAPTER SEVEN

As April drew closer, fewer and fewer pitches made that awful backstop-hitting sound. More and more smacked Mike's glove. It wasn't that my pitches ever became straight as arrows. It was just that Mike became crazy-good at blocking them. He'd leap to his left, dive to his right. He'd throw out a backhand to pick a pitch on the bounce. He'd kick out a leg to deaden a bouncer with his shin guards like a hockey goalie. He was ready. And okay, I did get better at pitching. My arm got stronger and my aim wasn't quite so wild. It was fun. I was proud. Who would have guessed that being a terrible pitcher would come in so handy? I felt happy that I could help. Sure, I still felt a little jealous that Mike was going to end up making the team and living the good life.

Yeah, I *was* sure that Mike was going to make the team. He was, you could say, not so sure. When the day of the Schwenkfelder Middle School base-ball tryouts arrived, Mike was just about nuts. It was a Monday. Mike was so nervous he could hardly sit still all day. He was so twitchy and fidgety you would have thought he was *Other* Mike. He invited me to come to the tryouts, but I thought that would just be weird.

We had spent the day before practicing—one last Sunday of wild pitches and impressive blocks. Every once in a while, I'd even throw a strike. Or, you know, something close enough to a strike that Mike could catch it without sprawling or diving like a fish. It made me feel good and it was good practice too. Mike wouldn't only need to catch wild pitches. That night, Mike had called, and I knew what he was going to say so well that I could mouth the words along with him into the phone.

"Lenny, think I'll make the team?"

"Of course," I said. "You're the best."

"Well, I'm not the best. I don't even need to be the best, not really. I just need to be the second best. I know the starting catcher's spot is Davis's—I know that. I just want to make it as a backup catcher. Is that too much to ask?"

I assured him that no, that was not too much to ask. It was a perfectly reasonable wish.

"Good luck," I said for the nine millionth time. "Break a mitt."

I decided to hang out with Other Mike after school during the tryouts. Our trio had been disrupted a little bit since I was spending so much time throwing wild pitches to Mike. I sort of missed Other Mike. He was never into baseball, but he was part of our crew since the beginning. He moved to Schwenkfelder from an even smaller town, if you can believe that. He was from the kind of place where a trip to a fast-food restaurant was a two-hour drive and a fancy night on the town. Mainly just farmland, I guess. I think his kindergarten class was mostly made up of cattle. So when he moved into our little neighborhood, he was thrilled to be in a place where, like, stuff existed. Where there were other kids around. It's just a little suburban neighborhood, but to Other Mike it was like moving to New York City.

I remember it well, the first day I met Other Mike. I don't know how he even found out where we lived—little-kid radar, I guess. Or maybe our moms talked. We were, like, in second grade. Anyway, there he was, walking up the street, just thrilled beyond belief to see me and Mike on the lawn. We were, of course, playing catch. We had our baseball gloves on and were hurling a ball back and forth. I was not catching it most times. I was not doing a good job throwing it most times either. Enough about that. So Other Mike ran up to us.

"Hi!" he said.

"Hey," Mike and I said in unison. We kept throwing the ball back and forth. We were too cool to stop. Except, you know, to pick up the ball because we were not catching it.

"I just moved here! My name is Mike!" Other Mike said.

"No it isn't," Mike said.

"Yeah, it is!" Other Mike was standing on the curb, still grinning.

"Nope," I said. We thought we were so funny.

"Okay, really it's Michael, but—"

"My name is Mike," Mike said. "There can't be two."

"Yeah," I said. "You're Other Mike." (Note: If you hear Mike tell this story, he'll try to take credit for being the one to make up "Other Mike," but it was totally me.)

Other Mike laughed. No one said anything else for a minute. "So are you into baseball?" he asked.

"What tipped you off?" Mike asked. We were such jerks!

"Yeah, we *are* into baseball," I said. "How about you?"

"Uh, sure," he said.

"Where did you move from?" Mike said. "What team are you into?"

Other Mike looked stumped for a minute. Stunned even. I saw him glance down at my Little League shirt. It had the team name on the front. That was the (one) year the coach let us pick our own name. We were the "Smashers." I don't know—it seemed cool at the time.

"Um, I'm into the . . . Smashers."

"Really?" Mike broke up laughing but wanted to keep the joke going. "Who is your favorite player on the Smashers?"

I doubled over with laughter.

Other Mike read the back of my shirt. "Norbeck?" he said.

"I like this kid already," I said.

He took it well. He admitted that he didn't like baseball. And we didn't care. He was fun, he was nice, and he was a good friend. Right from the beginning. He was *Other* Mike, but he was always himself. Can't beat that.

I was thinking about all this as I rode my bike over to Other Mike's house after school. Plus the fact that there were no video games at my house, of course, and I really wanted to play some.

Other Mike already was on the video-game machine. Before long we were having an epic battle in this really cool game Other Mike has where you're a ninja. I was climbing walls and stabbing dudes and chucking throwing stars. I lost track of time. When you don't play video games for a while, when you finally do it's like the greatest thing ever. It's like how when you're really hungry, even the cafeteria food tastes great. Just kidding. That never happened. The cafeteria food *always* stinks. But my point is, I was totally in the ninja zone and totally forgot what was going on in the real world. So when my phone beeped and I saw it was a text from Mike, I was sort of confused.

```
zo sez i'm a bench :) :) :)
```

"Dude," I said to Other Mike. "Pause it." He paused the game. "And answer me this: Does 'zo sez i'm a bench' mean anything to you?"

"Oh, it means *everything* to me," he said.

"Really?"

"No, I have no idea what that means," he said.

"I always thought Mike was more of a table than a bench."

Other Mike is annoying sometimes. He shook his hair out of his face and unpaused the game. "Stop it!" I said. "I'm not ready." I was about to text Mike back like "???" but then I figured it out. "Zo" is Coach Hinzo. Saying Mike is a "bench" means "Johnny Bench," one of the greatest catchers ever. He was the guy on the cover of Mike's weird *Become a Star Catcher!* book.

Did I feel my heart sink a little? Did I feel some sadness creeping in, there on the floor of Other Mike's living room? Maybe, sports fans. Just maybe. But I am a good friend. No matter what you've heard—*or what you will hear later*—don't ever forget that. I am a good friend.

I texted him back.

great!

And then resumed stabbing Other Mike with a samurai sword over and over and over again.

CHAPTER EIGHT

Let's just cut the suspense right here. I know it's killing you. So I'll get straight to it. Mike made the team. Davis Gannett was good and would start, but Coach Zo saw that Mike had the perfect skills to be a backup catcher. He could block every wild pitch, was an okay hitter, and could give Davis a break sometimes. It's hard catching every inning of every game, even if it's a pretty short season.

The list was posted outside the locker room on Friday. Tryouts were every day for that week, and every day was just about the same. I'd go over to Other Mike's house and spend a few hours killing people with swords. He'd talk about warlocks, I'd smile politely. I'd sort of hope that Mike would call or text with bad news—like he dropped forty-five pop-ups and had seven hundred passed balls—and then I'd feel bad about hoping for that. And that particular text never came. Each one was a glowing report by Coach Zo. There was no chance Mike wasn't going to make that team.

Still, he was so nervous you would have thought the odds were a million to one. You would have thought he was the Warlock Lontano attempting to remove the Sacred Ax of Daxeel from the Stone of Nevercede. Man, I might be hanging out with Other Mike too much.

"Dude," Mike said as we walked toward the gym that Friday afternoon. "Dude." It was basically all he could say. "Dude. Dude. Dude." He sounded like someone trying to start a lawn mower but it just wouldn't catch. I knew better than to try to talk too much. I simply walked along behind him. A good friend.

Then all of a sudden he started talking. "You know, Len, I really want to thank you for all that time pitching to me. No matter what happens. Just thanks."

"You're welcome, dude," I said.

Then he surprised me.

"You know, you should have gone out for the team too."

"What?" I said. "Remember who you're talking

to here. Lenny Norbeck. Old Norbs. The Human Rain Delay. Secretary of Being the Worst at Baseball in the History of the Known Universe."

"You were getting pretty good at pitching. And plus, you're pretty quick. You could pinch-run. Steal a few bases. Maybe come in to throw at guys we hate."

It is true. I *am* very fast. I have defeated my father in approximately eight hundred consecutive races. My exact record is eight hundred wins to three losses. But now that I think of it, he might have been letting me win at least a few of those. But what was up with those three? Was Dad just mad at me those days? I made a mental note to ask him.

"No," I said. "There's no way I'd make the team. But I'm glad to help."

So Mike made the team as the backup catcher. Then, day two into the preseason, the unthinkable happened. Actually, it wasn't that big of a surprise if I think about it. Honestly, it was rather thinkable. Totally thinkable. Here's how I got the news. I was at Other Mike's again after school, a few days before the season was set to start. We were in his room, playing ninjas on the video-game machine. And then a text from Mike came in.

```
dude, i might be evil for
saying this, but the best thing
ever just happened :) :) :)
```

I texted back something dumb like "Davis Gannett got hit by a truck?" And the funny thing was, that wasn't too far off. I don't mean he actually got hit by a truck. That would in fact have *not* been very funny. I don't even wish for guys like Davis Gannett to get hit by a truck. Perhaps a small car or a motorcycle maybe. Kidding, kidding. Mike's text came back:

```
no but he's off the team! :)
:) :) :)
```

Mike was kind of starting to overdo it with those smiley faces. But I got it. He was happy. How couldn't he be? Davis Gannett being off the team meant that the starting catcher was going to be none other than Mike DiNuzzio. I wondered what his baseball nickname would be. *DiNuzzio* didn't exactly work with the "first syllable rule." "Dins"? Maybe because it was pronounced Di-newts-ee-oh, they'd go with "Newts." Either that or "the Human Backstop." I just hoped that once he hit the big time, he'd remember where he came from.

I texted back:

whaaaaat?????

Which was the only possible appropriate response.

My first thought was that Davis couldn't keep his grades up above the rigorous standard of "adequate!" If you get all D's or worse, you can't do any sports or clubs. And it's not too hard to imagine Davis getting a report card full of "or worse." He'd probably pass gym, and quite possibly science, only because Mr. Daber is a big baseball fan. But otherwise, that kid could only dream of "adequate!" He thinks the square root is what you find at the bottom of a square tree. My second thought was that thing about getting hit by a truck, but Mike probably wouldn't have used so many smileys. Sure, we hated Davis, but that's just mean.

Mike texted back:

caught stealing :)

I thought it was pretty weird that Davis would get kicked off the team just for getting caught stealing once. Especially because the season hadn't started yet. What did he do, get picked off trying to steal second in a scrimmage? Or possibly, knowing Davis, Mike actually meant that he got caught stealing a cell phone. I texted this joke back to Mike and he was like:

how did you know???? :)

It turned out that Davis Gannett really did get caught stealing a phone! Apparently, it happened during practice. First baseman Kyle Webb's dad noticed his phone was missing. They're one of the richer families at school, so it was probably a pretty nice phone. Also, his dad is well known as being really mean.

Mr. Webb is the kind of guy who even comes to practices to cheer for his son. That is, "yell at his son." He's one of those red-faced, hollering dads who just constantly look like they're on their way to a heart attack. (That's the kind of thing your parents say if they're cardiologists.) Mr. Webb got really way too involved in Kyle's baseball career. Kyle wasn't bad at all. I mean, he was the starting first baseman and a pretty good hitter. But he was also one of the skinniest kids in school. His arms looked like threads hanging out of the end of his shirtsleeves. Mike's sister could beat him at arm wrestling. There was no chance Kyle was making the majors. He wasn't going to be on the Phillies anytime soon. Mr. Webb would disagree, but Mr. Webb had a problem with reality.

Anyway, I guess Mr. Webb left his phone on the bleachers and went to talk to Coach Zo (I mean "yell at Coach Zo") after the practice. He probably thought Kyle should be hitting higher in the batting order or something. The team was on their way back to the locker room, which meant that they would have to pass the bleachers. And after they did, the phone was gone.

Mr. Webb ran into the locker room and freaked out. I can only imagine the scene. He was probably beyond red into bright purple. He was probably punching lockers and kicking holes in the ceiling. I mean, not literally. Okay, maybe literally. Anyway, the missing phone was eventually found in Davis's gym bag, tucked into a shin guard. Davis of course insisted he had no idea how it got there. Yeah, right. Coach Zo didn't believe him. Coach Moyer didn't believe him. Mr. Webb didn't believe him. Nobody believed him. This is Davis Gannett we're talking about. He had a reputation for things far worse than petty theft. He was a good ballplayer, but there was no tolerance in Coach Zo's world for that sort of thing. Davis was kicked off the team immediately.

Getting this story over text from Mike was a little painful. And not just because of all of the smileys and misspellings. Because, let's be honest, I was jealous. Mike wasn't just going to make the team—he was going to be the starting catcher. Davis was gone. Coach Zo said he was a bench. I mean: a Bench! His new life began today. Was I a part of it?

"What's going on?" Other Mike asked. We were still in his room, the game paused. "Your phone's been going crazy. Did Coach Zo say that Mike was a table and a chair too?"

"Something like that," I said. "Something like that."

CHAPTER NINE

Before long, the first game of the Schwenkfelder Middle School baseball season had arrived. The first baseman was Kyle Webb. The starting catcher was Mike "Newts" DiNuzzio. And the starting pitcher was Hunter Ashwell. Mike had been going on and on about Hunter for weeks. Hunter Ashwell did this. Hunter Ashwell did that. Hunter Ashwell throws harder than anyone. Hunter Ashwell is so cool. Hunter Ashwell throws a sneaky palmball. Which is, okay, pretty cool.

The palmball is a great pitch. It oddly was not invented by the pitcher named Jim Palmer. Though coincidentally he did throw one sometimes. Other things I know about Jim Palmer from a library book I read: (1) His nickname was "Cakes," which is a terrible nickname. (2) He was an underwear model in the off-season, which is a really weird job for a baseball player (or anyone) to have in the off-season.

The palmball is pretty much like a changeup. Basically, you move your arm as fast as you would when throwing a fastball. But because you hold the ball back in your palm instead of up on your fingers, it comes out much slower. The batter sees you wind up hard—grunt and whip your arm around at full speed! But the ball comes out really slowly. The result, if done correctly, is a swing and a miss. Apparently, this was Hunter Ashwell's secret pitch and it made him Coach Zo's choice for opening day starter for Schwenkfelder.

Our opponent was Griffith Middle School. Griffith was located just about ten minutes away from Schwenkfelder and they were our biggest rivals. To be honest, they usually kicked our butts in most things. Griffith had a very good football team and an incredible basketball team. They might have even been better than "adequate!" when it came to academic stuff. But in baseball they were usually ours. And Mike was so excited that his first game behind the plate was going to be catching for the great Hunter Ashwell against the evil Griffith Griffins. Yes, their team name was the Griffith

Griffins. So dumb. Also, their color was green. I guess those guys love alliteration over there.

Mike spent the whole bus ride to school that morning literally bouncing up and down with excitement.

"It's our first game of the year!" he said.

"I know," I said.

"Hunter Ashwell is pitching," he said.

"I know," I said.

"Did I tell you that he throws a palmball?" he asked.

"Uh-huh," I said.

"We have this whole awesome secret system we made with Coach Zo so I can call the pitch and no one will know what's coming."

"He only throws two pitches," I said. "Doesn't have to be some genius system."

"Oh, Hunter is a genius," Mike said.

"I don't know if *genius* is the word I'd use," I said.

"He seriously is," Other Mike agreed.

"He's in my history class," I explained. "He thought that China and Japan were the same country. He absolutely refused to admit that they were different places. Even after we showed him a map."

"Well, he's a genius on the mound," Mike said.

"Somehow I doubt it."

"Come check it out. The first game of the year. Besides, there's a surprise for you."

"A surprise?" I said. "For me?"

"That's what I said."

"What is it?"

"If I told you, it wouldn't be a surprise."

I hate surprises. And I didn't want to go to the game. But I knew what being a good friend meant. I knew I had to be there. I just hoped this was like a present under the tree and not, you know, someone stealing all the presents from under the tree.

"Just be there early, Len," Mike said. "Coach Zo will be looking for you to go over a few things before the game."

I narrowed my eyes. What kind of surprise was he about to drop on me? Coach Zo was involved? Too weird.

"You better not have a cheerleader uniform with my name on it," I said.

"Baseball games don't have cheerleaders," Mike said. "And besides, cheerleaders don't have their names on their uniforms. Come on, Len, get your head in the game."

I should get *my* head in the game? Mike was acting weird.

After school I met up with Other Mike. He brought some reading material with him, but yeah, he was going to stay and watch the game too. I had already told the cardiologists that I would be staying after for the game. It was a home game, so it would be played just behind the school in the Schwenkfelder stadium. Well, "stadium" might be stretching it a bit. It's basically just a field with some metal bleachers. The field looked good, though—all sharply lined in fresh white chalk. And the grass looked extra green that day. The special green of grass on opening day. Could anything ruin it?

Well, yes.

We got to the field kind of early because of Mike's unclear statement about the "surprise." But when we arrived, all we found in the bleachers was Davis Gannett. I guess he wasn't in jail or even detention for his crime. He was just kicked off the team. And they couldn't keep him from coming to the game if he wanted. So there he was. He was the only one in the bleachers, and he looked like he had a storm cloud above his head. He looked like he *was* a storm cloud. His face was darkened and tight with anger. His fists were clenched into little balls. DO NOT MESS WITH ME was radiating off of him like stink lines in a cartoon.

So of course Other Mike went right up to him.

"Hey, Davis," he said. What was wrong with Other Mike???? Was that too many question marks? No! It was not nearly enough!!!!!!!!!!!!!!!!! Okay, now I might be overdoing it a bit, punctuation-wise. But didn't Other Mike remember that all Davis did was call us dork-buckets and threaten to poop in our milk cartons? And that also he was a thief and quite possibly a murderer? Or at least well on his way to becoming one?

Yet, oddly, Davis did not rip Other Mike's head off. He didn't even poop in his milk. Not that he was drinking milk, but you know what I mean. Maybe you don't. I'm not even sure I do. Anyway . . .

Davis actually looked like he was relaxing a little bit. I wouldn't say that his storm cloud of a face became a ray of sunshine, but he looked only *somewhat* likely to murder someone instead of *definitely* likely. He even unclenched his fists. I stayed nice and far away, in case Davis's mood shifted suddenly, but I was close enough to hear. I leaned up against a tree and pretended that I wasn't listening. I pretended to be just staring at the field, taking in the scenery.

"Hey, Davis," Other Mike repeated.

"What do you want, dork-bucket?"

"Nothing really. Just saying hello. Looking for a place to sit. Ready to watch the game? I'm not a fan, but I'm friends with Mike, so you know . . ."

"Yeah," Davis said with a scowl. "I *know*." He punched the metal bleacher he was sitting on. It made a loud ping that echoed through the air.

"What are you so mad about anyway?" Other Mike asked in his typical, clueless way.

"You wouldn't understand, dork-bucket," Davis said. "All you know is wizards and dragons."

"Technically they're warlocks, but I think I get your point. Doesn't really matter, though. I'm just asking."

"Yeah, well, why *wouldn't* I be mad? I should be out there catching this game—not your dork-bucket of a best friend," Davis said.

"Well," Other Mike said thoughtfully. "You do the crime, you do the time. That's what my dad always says."

Davis paused for a moment. "Your dad is doing time? Mine too. State or county?"

"What?" Other Mike laughed. Then he quickly covered his laughter. "No, not funny," he said. "I'm sorry. It's just that my dad is such a nerd, you know? I can't imagine him even jaywalking. He picks up *other* people's litter. That kind of a guy."

"I guess being a dork-bucket runs in the family," Davis said.

"Ha!" Other Mike said. "I suppose so. I suppose so."

They sat quietly for a moment, the two most improbable friends in the world. Like one of those picture books where a baby duck becomes best friends with a wolf and they teach us all the meaning of love. Then Davis leaned very, very close and said something very quietly to Other Mike that I couldn't hear. Other Mike nodded his head as if to say "Sure, sure, sure." I couldn't decide whether I should go join them or what. But before I could make up my mind, I heard a voice.

"There he is!" it boomed. "The boy with the golden voice."

I looked around, but couldn't see *where* the sound was coming from. Was he talking about me? "The Boy with the Golden Voice" was what Mike and Other Mike called me sometimes. I *am* a great announcer. But it was neither of them talking. The person talking, I was pretty sure, was Coach Zo.

He continued. "That's right, Lenny Norbeck, I'm talking to you!"

CHAPTER TEN

Somehow I had completely missed it! Right next to the dugout was a little building made out of wood and painted Schwenkfelder maroon. A Plexiglas window faced the field. And inside the Plexiglas was Coach Zo. Speaking into a microphone. I knew immediately what it was, and I knew immediately who was behind it. Mike's dad had built an announcer's booth for the middle school!

I ran over, forgetting immediately about the conversation Other Mike was having with his new BFF Davis Gannett. Mike was in the booth too, wearing his uniform and smiling. There wasn't much room for anyone else.

"So what do you think?" Mike asked.

"Well, you know," I said, teasing. "It's not quite as luxurious as what I'm used to, but it ain't bad." It really was a tiny little room, basically the dimensions of a shed. Coach Zo couldn't stand up straight or he'd whack his head. He was very tall. Coach Zo was just a big guy. Even though he was over the hill, he had the height and build of a ballplayer. He looked like he could grab a bat and go out there and hit one four hundred feet. Stooped into the announcer's booth, he looked like an old man, but Coach Zo was a beast.

He smiled and handed me the microphone. "Newts here said you had some experience with this sort of thing. I didn't know we had such a talent in the school. I mean—I knew you were a heck of a detective. I heard all about what happened at the Phils last year. Very impressive. I'm a detective fan myself. Agatha Christie, that kind of thing. Hercule Poirot has got nothing on you, though, kid."

Awesome! Coach Zo was a legend and he was complimenting *me*.

He continued. "So Mike and his dad asked me if they could build this for you. They said you're the one responsible for turning Newts here into a catcher. So thanks for that. They have been coming in after practice and working on this thing until it got dark. Pretty cool."

"That *is* pretty cool!" I said. Because it was.

And also it was pretty cool that "Newts" was catching on as Mike's nickname just as I predicted. Maybe I'd be able to give everybody nicknames! Oh, the power of the announcer! I could name Hunter Ashwell something like "Ash-smell." . . . Though, wait, that's probably not good. "Do I get a color commentary guy?" I asked. Every play-by-play announcer gets a retired big leaguer or wacky personality to sit next to him and make weird comments.

"Oh no," Coach Zo said. "You're not . . . Well, you can't do play-by-play really. The league has rules. You'll be more of the in-game-type guy. The PA announcer. 'Now coming to the plate . . .' That sort of thing."

"Oh." I shrugged. Not *quite* as cool. But still I couldn't pass it up. There would be nickname possibilities. And I'd get to be part of the game, if not part of the team.

"That is," Coach Zo said, "if you're interested."

"How much do I get paid?" I asked.

"Nothing," Coach said.

"Double it and you've got yourself a deal," I said.

"I'll triple it," he said, sticking out his hand.

Ah, multiplication jokes. We shook on it. "When do I start?"

"Today, if you're up for it," Coach said. "Game starts in a few minutes. I have the lineups here so you'll know who is who on both squads." He handed me a couple of printouts with names and numbers and positions for the Schwenkfelder Mustangs and the Griffith Griffins. "Just keep it simple—announce the name of the batter as he comes up to the plate. If there's a pitching change, announce the new guy. Nothing fancy."

"Got it," I said. "Simple. Nothing fancy is my middle name."

"Uh, thanks," he said, giving me an odd look.

"Oh, thank you," I said. "And thanks to you too, Newts."

Before it got too sappy of a manly moment in that little announcer's shed (it really was more of a shed than a booth), Other Mike came in.

"You're just like the hobbit in here!" he said to me. "Sweet hobbit-hole. Invite me in for elevenses sometime."

"Um, thanks?" I asked.

"You are welcome," he said. Apparently, being the hobbit is a good thing?

Mike and Coach Zo squeezed past him. They had pregame prep to do. I had my own work to do! I had to learn how to operate the microphone, first of all! Well, okay, it wasn't that hard. It basically just had one button that you pressed to talk. It was a cool mike, though—kind of old-fashioned-looking. I thought about my old friend Buck Foltz, the great Phillies announcer. Maybe he got his start like this? Probably not, because he was so old that he probably got his start shouting through one of those cone things. But anyway, this was an extremely cool chance to be back in the announcer's seat. It was really nice of Mike.

I had some other work to do too, mainly figuring out how to pronounce the names of the guys on the teams! I knew everyone from Schwenkfelder, and even knew how to say relief pitcher Henry Hrab. Hint: The *H* is silent. I mean in *Hrab*. You do say the *H* in *Henry*. What did you think, his name was *Enry*? I scanned the list. There were some tough ones for Griffith, including a pitcher named Jagdish Sheth. No offense, J-dog, but I sort of hoped you didn't get into the game.

But something was still bothering me from before.

"Hey, Other Mike," I said. "What on earth were

you talking about with our dear friend Davis Gannett over there?"

Other Mike was tapping on the Plexiglas window of the booth, muttering, "Precious . . . My precious . . ."

"Other Mike!" I said louder, to snap him out of it.

"Huh, what?" he said.

"What were you talking about with Davis?"

"Nothing. He was saying that he was mad he got kicked off the team, stuff like that. Oh, and he said his dad was in jail. Or is in jail. Not really sure. Not really surprised either."

"No," I said. "I heard that part. I meant the other part. Right before Coach Zo started talking into the microphone." This reminded me to quickly check to make sure that the microphone was off. That kind of thing was always happening to politicians and celebrities. They'd forget that a mike was live and they'd start talking about which countries they were going to bomb or which of their friends they hated. I *had* to make sure that never happened to me. Not that I secretly hated any of my friends. And not that I had any countries I wanted to bomb. Though, to be honest, Kyrgyzstan was kind of getting on my nerves. Only because we had to learn how to spell it for social studies. Ridiculous. Stupid Kyrgyzstan, why can't you be more like Chad?

But anyway, I did *not* want the microphone on while I secretly talked about Davis Gannett. The last thing I needed was to give him a reason to beat me up. I double-checked, then triple-checked. The mike was off.

"Oh," Other Mike said. "Davis was just saying that he did *not* steal Kyle Webb's dad's phone. He said someone else did it."

"That doesn't make sense," I said. "They found the phone in *Davis's* shin guard. Who else could it have been who took it? Who else would steal a phone by putting it in Davis's shin guard?"

"That's just the point, isn't it?" Other Mike said. "They weren't trying to steal it. They were trying to frame Davis."

I tapped the microphone with the tip of my finger a few times. "He said all that in the, like, two seconds you were talking?" I said.

"Well," Other Mike said. "That was the basic idea. I'm filling in a lot of the blanks. Davis mostly talks in grunts and snorts. It's like talking to a caveman, kind of. He just said it wasn't him who took the phone, ugh, grunt, snort. Just showed up there. Ugh, sniff, burp. I filled in the blanks. You're not the only one who has detective skills." He smiled and tapped his head.

"Oh, I know it," I said. "Remember when we were little and used to pretend to be spies, gathering information on everyone in the neighborhood?"

"You were pretending?" he said.

I laughed. "Yeah," I said. "So who would want to frame Davis?"

"Beats me," Other Mike said. "I get the feeling that everyone kind of hates him."

"Imagine that," I said. I tried to remember if I'd seen Davis torment anyone in particular at school besides us. He was pretty much an equal opportunity tormentor, but there were a few guys he really bothered I could name. I was going to run this theory by Other Mike, but although he does have some detective skills, he is also sort of ADD.

"Hey, what does this do?" he said, reaching over and flicking the microphone's On switch. It was pretty obvious what it did, seeing as how it said ON in big red letters.

"Stop it!" I yelled, and smacked his hand, but it was too late. He'd already turned it on. The microphone made a loud squealing sound and everyone could hear me yell. Coach Zo turned quickly and stared over at us. Great, I was going to get fired before the first pitch was even thrown!

"Sorry!" Other Mike said, flicking the switch back off.

"Yeah, a lot of people don't like Davis," I started to say. "But he made the team so much better that I figure they'd just put up with it to win a championship. The only person I can think of who could really stand to gain from Davis getting kicked off the team was—"

But before I could finish that thought, Coach Zo came running over. He stuck his head into the shed. "We're just about to get started. I forgot to show you this." He handed me a portable CD player. "It's got a disc loaded up already with the national anthem on it. All you have to do is press Play and hold it up to the mike. Start it when I give you the signal."

"Got it, Coach," I said. I had so much power. The power to start the game! The very anthem of this very nation rested in my very hands!

Of course I also had the power to solve mysteries.

But did I want to?

CHAPTER ELEVEN

Coach Zo gave me the signal, and after a brief second of fumbling I found the Play button. The On switch I already knew how to find. I gently flipped it on. A loud brass-band version of the national anthem began to blare out of the booth. I guess Mike's dad had installed speakers around the field. He must have buried speaker wire and gotten some rainproof speakers, not to mention all the time and effort and expense of putting together the actual booth. Shed. Whatever. It was really nice. Mike was a nice friend. A good person. Not a bad person. Not a bad person at all, right? Right.

These thoughts were running through my head as the recorded brass band hit the final home-of-the-brave high notes at the end of the anthem. The umpire yelled, "Play ball!" and the game was begun. The season was begun. I got goose bumps.

They really should have given me some time to practice. I had questions. Like, was I supposed to announce the starting pitcher? Coach Zo only said to announce if there was a pitching *change*, but in the first inning . . . I just decided to go for it. Thankfully, I was an old pro at this sort of thing.

"Pitching for the Schwenkfelder Mustangs," I said in my booming announcer's voice, "number twenty-five, Hunter Ashwell." There was wild applause, presumably all for me. The leadoff batter for Griffith was named Jaxon Sadler. Jaxon? I hoped I pronounced it right. Why did people always have to go sticking random *x*'s and *q*'s into names? Thankfully, Jaxon fouled off a few pitches, which gave me a bit more time to get acclimated and to scan the lineup card and get used to the names. Then he struck out on a wicked palmball and I had to bite my tongue. I couldn't yell out "Whiff!" or anything like that. Just announce the batters and pitching changes. That's it.

There was also a guy on the Griffith team, no lie, named Trebor. Trebor Fenner. His twin brother was named Robert Fenner. How mean. To have twins and give one of them a regular name like Robert and then the other one a name like Trebor? Poor Trebor. And poor me! How are you supposed to pronounce that? Tree-boar? Treb-or? I thought about just going with *Fenner* when he came up, but there were two of them. I went with *Tree-boar*. Sounded kind of cool, really. Some sort of wild animal. Like a, uh, boar. That lived in a tree.

It didn't really matter how anyone on Griffith spelled their names. They might as well all have spelled them with nothing but *K*'s. *K* is the baseball term for strikeout. My point is, Jaxon, both Fenners, and even Jagdish Sheth were hopeless against Hunter Ashwell. (Jagdish came in to pitch in the third inning after their starter got hit around a bit. He stayed in to bat, but whiffed mightily. I mumbled his name a little bit and hoped he'd forgive me.)

Hunter Ashwell really was an amazing pitcher! He just had those two pitches—the fast one and the slow palmball. But the way he threw them, you could never tell what was coming. Everyone was always hacking really early or really late. You would have thought that they'd make contact half the time just by guessing, but he always kept them off-balance. *Mike* kept them off-balance. He was a genius at knowing which pitch to call and when. When the hitters did make contact, it was weak contact. Hunter was unstoppable.

I started to have visions of Hunter Ashwell pitching in the big leagues. It was kind of funny to ponder because Hunter Ashwell didn't look like much. He had braces and the same swoopy haircut I mentioned a lot of the kids had. Hunter was on the short side and maybe they ran out of uniforms that fit him, because every bit of his Schwenkfelder maroons hung a few inches long. He was basically swimming in the shirt and the pants. Even the hat seemed oversized for his small head. Maybe he was one of those short guys who refused to admit that he was little and couldn't let himself mark S on the S-M-L sheet they hand out when you have to sign up for uniforms. He insisted on being a large, never mind all the evidence to the contrary.

Hunter also seemed to be having visions of himself as a big-league pitcher. He'd hoot and hol-ler after every strikeout, yelling stuff like "Sit down, sucker!" and "I am the *man!*" If it was physically possible to high-five yourself while wearing a base-ball glove, I'm pretty sure he would have done that too. He struck out just about every Griffin to grab a bat. Okay, not *every* batter, but the vast majority of them whiffed big-time. The few that made con-tact just dribbled grounders or hit weak pop-ups that were easily caught.

The only drama was when Kyle Webb dropped a pop-up, but it was a foul ball, so the batter didn't reach base. The batter had to get back there and swing again, which he did far too early. Palmball, strike three. Kyle's dad seemed really mad about it, though. I could hear him screaming at his son from the bleachers. Kyle looked pretty sad. His dad was such a red-faced maniac. He was angrier than that girl in the Olympics who spent her whole life training for the vault, then fell on her butt on national TV. And that was the Olympics! This was just middle school sports. And a *foul ball*. I had the distinct feeling that there was something wrong with Mr. Webb and I felt really bad for Kyle. But it didn't affect the game.

It was already the fourth inning when I realized that no one on Griffith had reached base. Schwenkfelder had scored a ton. There is a "mercy rule," which means that the game is called after five innings if one team is winning by ten. It's also known as the "run rule" or, more often and unofficially, the "whoop rule." As in "Schwenkfelder put the whoop on Griffith."

I know the big leagues don't have the whoop rule (sorry, Houston Astros!), but it was still pretty amazing that Hunter had a chance at the perfect game. A perfect game! It's really hard, one of the rarest events in all of baseball. The pitcher has to be, well, perfect. No walks, no runs, no hit batters. Even your fielders have to be perfect because an error can ruin a perfect game. Seems unfair, but that's baseball. That's life. That's why the perfect game is so rare.

Hunter struck out all three guys in the top of the fourth just about as quickly as I could announce their names. Boom, boom, boom. Schwenkfelder came up to bat in the bottom of the inning and tacked on a few more runs. Mike struck out for the third time of the day. Everyone was getting hits except him, so I wondered if he felt bad. But he didn't seem to. He was focused on being a good catcher, and he was doing a great job.

All that remained was the top of the fifth. Just three batters left for the perfecto. You could feel everyone get a little tense. (Well, everyone except for Other Mike, who sat in the booth next to me. I wasn't quite sure he grasped the enormity of the situation, but it was nice having him there.)

The first batter up got ahead in the count after Hunter threw two fastballs very high. You couldn't blame him for pushing a little bit. It was getting exciting. No one mentioned the perfect game to him, as baseball superstition insists. You just can't mention it. It's considered a jinx. It's like how you can't tell an actor "Good luck." You have to say "Break a leg." So no one said anything. It got to a point that no one was talking to Hunter at all. Everyone avoided him like he was carrying a rare and deadly disease. It seemed to shake him up.

Mike walked out to the mound to settle him down, just like a good catcher should. The batter must have thought it meant he was going to throw the slow one because he waited on the next pitch, but it was a heater right down the middle. He couldn't even get his bat off his shoulder. The next pitch *was* the slow one, but all the batter could do was manage a foul tip.

Unfortunately for Mike, the foul tip made the ball hit the plate and bounce right up into his crotch. He shrugged it off. As for me, his good friend and practice crotch-kicker, I felt proud. Despite the rule against in-game commentary, I came up with a funny line I couldn't resist.

"Oooh," I said. "Right in the newts."

That evened the count to two balls (ahem) and two strikes. The umpire threw the ball back to Hunter to give Mike a moment to recover. There's a subtle brotherhood between catcher and umpire, the two masked men behind the plate. Hunter caught the ball, then took a little walk behind the mound. He hitched up his belt. He wiped some sweat off his forehead. He stepped back onto the mound. He wound up and fired strike three: pure smoke.

The next batter was Trebor Fenner. The twins were both little guys with identical everything, including haircuts. Well, the part you could see under their hats was identical. Both hadn't been to Benderson in many years, I knew that. A stream of long, straight black hair shot out of the back of their caps. They both wore identical scowls on their faces as well. These Fenners meant business. You could tell they wanted nothing more than to spoil Hunter's perfect game.

Being amped up isn't really a good frame of mind to enter a batter's box in. Especially against Hunter. Hunter was the master at making the pitch look like it was going to be a million miles an hour but instead having it creep in as slow as a turtle. He threw his turtle ball three times against poor Trebor, and with each pitch Trebor swung earlier and earlier. Strike one, strike two, strike three. It looked like Trebor wanted to bend his aluminum bat in half, Superman-style, as he walked back to the dugout.

The final batter was the other Fenner twin, Robert. Robert clearly didn't want to repeat Trebor's overanxious hacking. He took a *long* time walking to the plate. He tapped the dirt off his cleats. He spit into his gloves. He spit on the ground. He spit on the bat. He was running out of places to spit. I knew what he was doing. He was trying to psych Hunter out. He was trying to break his rhythm, mess up his concentration. I wanted so bad to yell something rude at him. And believe me, knowing I had a microphone in front of me did not make it easier to resist. But I was good. I said nothing other than "Now batting for Griffith, Robert Fenner." Okay, I said it about four times, each time with more and more annoyance, but that was all I said. Eventually I was screaming "NOW BATTING FOR GRIFFITH, ROBERT FENNER!"

Finally Robert stepped into the box. Then he held up his hand to call for time. There was a collective groan from the audience. There might have been one from the announcer's booth too. He stepped out of the batter's box and started messing with his gloves. Then the umpire got annoyed and screamed, "Quit farting around!" This got a good laugh from the crowd. Robert was not amused. Nor was the Griffith coach, who, if I wasn't mistaken, had to be Mr. Fenner. He had the same intense eyes as the twins. And also he kept calling Robert "son." I'm a really good detective.

Robert narrowed his eyes and dug in at the plate. Mike gave the sign. Hunter went into his windup, and fired a fastball. Robert guessed correctly this time. He was swinging fastball all the way. The ball exploded off the bat, flying high and deep down the left-field line. But he was a fraction of a second too early and hooked it foul and out of play.

"Just a long strike," I could hear Mike say from behind the plate. "Long strike. Means nothing. We got this."

He gave the sign again, and again came the fastball. Robert didn't see it coming this time and didn't even get his bat off his shoulder. Right down the middle. Strike two. One out away from the promised land. Hunter had to be so full of adrenaline. Everyone in the stadium felt another fastball coming. Which was why it was the perfect time to call for the slow one. Hunter bore down like he wanted to throw the heater through Mike's glove, through Mike's body even. Through the umpire and through the backstop. But instead: the slowest slowball that ever slowed. Even time slowed. You could hear Robert blink a few times. And you could hear the air as he swung and missed. A big whiff for strike three! A perfect game! Six strikeouts in a row to end it!

Mike caught the ball, threw his mask off, and charged the mound. It was a move I'd seen on TV many times. Every no-hitter and lots of big wins end with the catcher flipping off his mask and charging the mound. It was a baseball cliché. But still, it was awesome. Every single time. And this time it was Mike getting to be the catcher, holding the ball up like a trophy and charging the mound. He hugged Hunter, then the rest of the team swarmed in, a sea of maroon jerseys swamping the little pitcher.

Everyone was cheering and having a good time. Well, not the guys on Griffith of course. And not one guy in the crowd on the Schwenkfelder side: Davis Gannett.

As for me, I was pumped. I knew I was just supposed to announce the batters as they came up and give the info on new pitchers. But the game was officially over, wasn't it? Couldn't I add my own thoughts now that the game was over? I figured I could. I couldn't resist anyway. I cleared my throat, grabbed the microphone, and boomed my voice with its most epic sound possible, saying whatever came to mind.

"*Star of the game is of course Hunter Ashwell, who pitched very well. That's an understatement. Extremely well. Perfectly well. One for the record books. Perfection is not easy to do. That's why they call it perfection, sports fans. Hunter, you struck out the last six consecutive batters and retired fifteen in a row from first man to last. Not a single player reached base. On the scoreboard in center field here in the city of Schwenk stands nothing but zeroes, like a half dozen eggs on the shelf. What a performance. You wrote your name in capital letters in the record books today, Hunter Ashwell. Yes, you did.*"

I didn't add that Hunter only knew how to write in capital letters, never having mastered the intricacies of lowercase, much less cursive. I figured I'd leave that part out. It was a good place to end it. "Lenny Norbeck, signing off," I said. Had to add that little bit there.

Hunter then ran over to the announcer's booth and climbed inside. I thought he was going to give me a high five, but he wanted the microphone. He grabbed it out of my hands and turned it on. He started talking about himself in the third person. "I can't say enough about the great job Ashwell did out there," he said, all out of breath. "I mean, did you *see* him out there, people of Schwenkfelder? He really threw a great game. He just took *over* out there. Hot diggity doggity dig, he did a great job. I mean a *great* job! Who is the greatest pitcher in the world, I ask you? The answer is a no-brainer. It is I, the destroyer of worlds! I just go out, see the glove, and hit it. Boom. Ashwell out." He dropped the microphone.

I didn't add any commentary about every day being a no-brainer for Hunter. I just said, "And way to go, Newts, for calling a great game!" to much applause. There was applause for quite a while. Mike smiled and smiled. Hunter just looked annoyed and made a noise that sounded like *ew*. I was beginning to suspect that he wasn't a great teammate. Then Coach Zo announced that we were all going out for pizza! I got really excited for a second and then remembered that I wasn't on the team. Coach Zo saw me pump my fist and laughed.

"Sure, Lenny," he said. "Of course you can come too." Good guy, that Coach Zo. I called my parents and told them I was going out with the team and that I'd be home late. Dad seemed surprisingly okay with it. He wasn't too excited about my dream to be a baseball announcer, but I think it was starting to sink in that I'd never be a doctor.

I rode to Ralph's Pizza with the Newts family. Mike's mom and dad were so proud. It made me a little jealous. I wished my parents were celebrating my excellent announcing.

The pizza bash at Ralph's was raucous and fun. The only bummer was that I sat next to Kyle Webb, who seemed depressed.

"What's wrong, dude?" I asked in between mouthfuls of pizza. "You guys won. Perfect game."

"My dad totally embarrassed me out there," he said.

"Nah," I said. "No one even noticed. Besides, it was just a foul ball."

"See!" he said. "You *did* notice. That was a really bad lie, Lenny. You just pretended that you didn't notice and then described the exact thing you were pretending not to notice."

"Oh yeah," I said, and shrugged. I didn't want to get bummed down into Webb-land. It was not a fun time. But Kyle kept talking.

"I wish my mom would have been there too.

She's the real baseball fan. But they're divorced. They have to, like, take turns which one sees me when. My dad isn't himself anymore. He used to be fun. Now he yells all the time. If you thought dropping a foul ball was bad, you should see him when I forget to feed the dog. I wish they never got divorced."

"Your dad got divorced from the dog?" I say. Trying to make a dumb joke. Keep it light.

"I wish," Kyle said.

I didn't know what to say to that.

Kyle continued. "It's bad. My parents hate each other."

"Yeah," I said, not sure what else to say at all. "Gotta be rough."

This conversation reminded me that I was lucky to have two parents who essentially did care about me. And who didn't fight all the time.

It was a strange feeling, sitting there at Ralph's Pizza watching the team have a good time. Hunter was living it up. Mike had a smile so wide it looked like it might break his face. So did his parents. Coach Zo was laughing and relaxing with Coach Moyer. And yet there was Kyle Webb, almost in tears.

The world was a strange place sometimes.

CHAPTER TWELVE

The next game was against Highland Middle School. Highland was farther away than Griffith, and too far to ride my bike. I wanted to go along, even though I wouldn't be working. I thought it would be a good opportunity to scout out the other team and get a sense of what we were up against. Yes, I know it's weird that sometimes I would say "we" when talking about the team. I knew I wasn't on the team. But people around here pretend they're on the Phillies all the time. You hear it on the radio constantly. It's always "We need a better bullpen" or "We need to bunt more." And at least I actually go to the school. And work for the team. Sort of.

So I asked Coach Zo if I could ride on the bus. Games start at five-thirty and my parents never get home until after that. If it was up to my parents, I'd just come home from school on the bus and lock myself in the house alone, watching TV. Actually, they probably would prefer it if I was doing my homework, but we all know that isn't going to happen!

Coach Zo said it would be fine. Wonderful even. He said they would consider it an honor to have my presence and that I was the good-luck charm for the whole team. Actually, he said, "Sure, whatever, Lenny." But we all know what he meant.

The bus ride to Highland was fun. The team was feeling great. How could they not be? You literally could not ask for a better start to the season. A ten-to-nothing whoop of Griffith and a perfect game to boot. Pretty sweet. I sat in the middle of the bus, next to Mike. Hunter sat in the seat behind us. He kept wanting to talk about the game, over and over again. I could understand, sure, but he was getting so cocky it was hard to listen to.

"I have an idea for a new nickname for myself," he said.

"Um, you're not supposed to give yourself nicknames," I said. "Duh. Everybody knows that."

Mike laughed, knowing my years-long track record of trying to get a cool nickname.

"From here on out, I want to be called the Great Imperial Ashwell," he said.

Mike and I looked at each other, narrowing our eyes. "Um, I'm not sure the Great Imperial Ashwell is the kind of nickname you should give yourself," Mike said.

"It's also not that catchy," I added. "Hard to print on a T-shirt."

"Man, let the T-shirt makers figure that out their own selves. The Great Imperial Ashwell has more important things to worry about. Like what the name should be for my new pitch. I'm thinking about calling it the Great Imperial Ashwell's Destroyer of Worlds."

"Definitely pretty catchy," I said. "Do you really have a new pitch?"

Hunter laughed. "Yeah, man, I got new pitches every day. I got the Bat Dodger, Midnight Rider, Midnight Creeper, Midnight Streaker, Midnight Weeper. I got the Jump Ball, Trouble Ball, and Bee-Bee Ball. That's just getting started."

Mike rolled his eyes and whispered to me, "He really only has two pitches. Sometimes he throws his fastball extra hard, but I'm not really sure it deserves its own name."

"The Great Imperial Ashwell has hundreds of

pitches!" Hunter roared. He cackled like a super-villain.

Mike and I laughed. Everyone laughed. Well, not Kyle Webb, who was the world's saddest first baseman. The divorce—or something else—really seemed to be bothering him.

"Settle down," Coach Zo said. "We got a game to think about. This team is no joke."

Highland Middle School actually *was* a joke. Everyone knew that. First of all, there were no highlands around it. It was just flat farm country. So it kind of was a joke. It was like the Pleasant Valley Mall in that regard, which was neither in a valley nor pleasant. It really was a mall, though. Sort of.

More to the point, Highland's baseball team wasn't really great. Everyone knew that too. One year they managed to come in fourth in a three-team league. No one is quite sure how they pulled that off. It was a record of futility sure to stand the test of time. Kind of like my new favorite baseball player I read about in a library book: Bill Bergen. He was a catcher, mostly for the Reds and also the Superbas. That's right, there was a team called "the Superbas." They're now the Dodgers, which is also a weird name if you think about it. Anyway, Bill

Bergen played, like, a hundred years ago. And he got five hundred hits in his career. Which sounds like a lot, except for that he had a really long career. He had three thousand at bats! Five hundred hits over three thousand at bats is pretty bad. His batting average was about .170. Really bad.

The entire Highland team was basically a bunch of Bill Bergens. Actually, they wished they were Bill Bergen. From where they sat, a batting average of a buck seventy was, like, all-star caliber.

The energy was high and everyone was in great spirits as we rolled into the parking lot. The team went into the locker room to get dressed for the game and to warm up. I thought about finding the Highland PA announcer to introduce myself and talk about the tools of the trade. But they didn't even have a PA booth. Losers! I realize that we didn't have one until a week ago, but still, it made me feel superior to Highland. It also meant that I needed something else to do before the game began. I was all on my lonesome. Other Mike had not been in the least interested in making the trip, and everyone else here went to Highland (duh).

Then I saw a familiar face trudging up the path toward the field. It was Davis Gannett.

CHAPTER THIRTEEN

I tried to ignore Davis. I just pretended he wasn't there. Like, I knew he saw me, and I knew he knew I saw him. I knew he knew that I saw him seeing me. And he knew that I was trying to pretend not to see him just as I knew he was pretending not to see me. It was very complicated. But the basic agreement was that we each pretend the other wasn't there.

The warm-ups were over and the team was getting ready for the game. Coach Zo was busy talking to the umpires and the coach for Highland, so there was a bit of a lull. Mike walked over to the bleachers where I was sitting and flipped up his catcher's mask. I walked down to the chain-link fence to talk to him.

"Hey," he said.

"Hey," I said. "Did you see who's here? Don't look."

"How am I supposed to see who is here without looking?"

"I mean, look but don't look. Fine, I'll just tell you. It's Davis Gannett."

"What?" Mike said, whipping his head around.

"I told you not to look!"

"What is he doing here?" Mike asked.

"Beats me. I guess his mom dropped him off. Did you know that his dad's in jail?"

"Runs in the family, I guess," Mike said. "Seriously, what is he doing here?"

"Just watching the game, I guess," I said.

"Well, keep an eye on him," Mike said.

"I will," I said. "I will."

The game was ready to start. There are rules in middle school about how many innings a pitcher can pitch, so Hunter wasn't going to start this one. He was under his limit for the week because the game against the Griffith Griffins had ended early, and of course he insisted that he be allowed to throw. "The more I pitch, the stronger my arm gets!" he said. Which is totally not true. You need to rest your arm. Everyone knows that. In the old days, guys would throw five hundred innings. But then their shoulders would break and their arms would fall off. These days everyone is very concerned with pitch count. Especially for young guys. The limit was seven innings a week and even that was considered a stretch.

So the starting pitcher for the Schwenkfelder Mustangs would be Byron Lucas. I knew Byron from a few of my classes. He was a tall kid known around here for being a great basketball player. He was a pretty good pitcher too, a hard-throwing lefty with a habit of pitching inside. Maybe it was intentional, maybe it wasn't. It worked, though. Guys were afraid to dig in against him, not wanting to catch a heater in the ear. Can't say that I blamed them. I was bummed that I wouldn't get to call the game because "Byron Lucas" seemed like it would be a fun thing to yell into the microphone. I kept saying it in my head. *Byrrrrrrron Luuuuuuuucas.*

I found a place on the small set of bleachers as far away from Davis as possible and watched the game. Schwenkfelder was the visiting team, of course, so we batted first. Cason Pearce, our center fielder, was first up. He lined a single to left-center but promptly got thrown out trying to stretch it to a double. The whole game was like that—back and forth. Something good would happen, then something bad would happen. Coach Zo looked like he wanted to tear out what little hair he had left on his head.

Mike did a good job as catcher. Nothing got past him and he even got a hit. Of course, right after his hit, Kyle Webb grounded into a double play.

I noticed that Kyle's crazy dad wasn't in the bleachers, so at least he didn't have to deal with that. I did hear a loud cheer when he came up to bat, though, so it had to be his mom. That must be so weird, having your parents have to take turns. Like they can't even be in the same room together. Same stadium. Whatever.

Byron pitched pretty well. He was nothing like Hunter. He was hittable. Actually, the first batter got a hit, ruining the perfect game. There were a few more hits in there, and one monster blast. A huge kid on Highland named Chad Fine smacked a home run that might still be traveling to this day. It tied the game, where it remained going into the seventh.

Middle school games only have seven innings. So it was tense. The Highland pitcher was still in there, going for the complete game. His seventh inning of the week. The more he pitched, the stronger he seemed to get. He was in a pretty good groove. So they left him in for the top of the seventh.

Bad move on their part.

The top of the seventh started with a walk. A walk is never a good way to start an inning, as the announcers always say. Cason Pearce walked on four pitches. The next batter, Reece Burns, tapped a grounder to first, which moved Cason to second. He moved to third on a wild pitch that squiggled away from the Highland catcher. (Mike totally would have blocked it.) Our number-three hitter, left fielder Wade Hartman, lifted a fly ball to center and Cason scored. A nice manufactured run. The team rejoiced in the dugout. The tide was turning. But the big pitcher from Highland seemed angered by it and promptly struck the next two batters out.

That led to a one-run lead heading into the bottom of the seventh.

"Bottom of the seventh" doesn't sound as dramatic as "bottom of the ninth," but trust me, it was dramatic. I announced in my head, giving the commentary on the situation.

Bottom of the seventh with Schwenkfelder holding

a one-run lead at four to three. Coach Zo has elected to keep starter Byron Lucas in to finish the game. He's pitched pretty well and seems strong enough to do it. Plus, with two lefties due up for Highland, the matchup favors keeping the tall southpaw in the game.

But leading off is a righty, the shortstop they call Zach. Zach digs in and takes ball one low and outside. Zach has two hits today and is looking for his third. The second pitch is high and outside. He'll take a walk too if one's offered up on a platter. Highland's looking for base runners. Lucas is looking to limit them. Here's the pitch—ball three. Lucas quickly behind. And he follows it up with ball four. That's a four-pitch walk to lead off the inning. Not a good way to start the inning for the Mustangs. Coach Zo is pacing the dugout, wiping the sweat dripping from his nose.

The next batter is the lefty first baseman everyone keeps calling Huffman.

(It's hard being the announcer without knowing the players' names. And since they don't have a PA announcer like we do, I just had to guess from what people were saying in the stands.)

Huffman will make Lucas throw strikes here. . . .

But Byron *couldn't* throw strikes. Okay, he did get a few over, which Huffman fouled off.

You have to hand it to Huffman. He's fouling off

some tough pitches. Lucas is battling. The count is full. Here's the windup, and the pitch, and . . . ball four! He walks him. Highland now has two men on and nobody out. It looks like Coach Zo is going to give Lucas one more chance.

He'll be pitching against Highland's number-three hitter, Bo Hertzman. Hertzman is one for three on the day. He's probably going to take a pitch here, to see if Lucas can throw a strike. Here's the windup, and the pitch. . . . It hits him! Hertzman takes a fastball to the foot. Boy, that hurts. He shakes it off and heads to first. That's bases loaded with nobody out, here in the bottom of the seventh.

You gotta think that's it for Lucas. He's battled today. Gave his team a chance to win. That's all you can ask. He'll leave with the lead, still in line for the win. But he'll also leave with the bases loaded, no outs, and the hard-hitting Chad Fine stepping into the dish. The question remains—who will Coach Zo bring into the game?

And there's your answer! Heading out to the mound is he of the perfect game. None other than Hunter Ashwell. Ashwell will have his hands full here, trying to retire Fine and the next three batters while preserving a lead.

Catcher Mike DiNuzzio will have his hands full as

well. A passed ball or a wild pitch will no doubt result in the tying run scoring. Sompel on third looks like he has some speed. He could score easily if the ball gets past the catcher. Good thing Newts had all that practice with his good friend Lenny Norbeck, who also happens to be the greatest announcer in the world.

Ashwell steps to the mound and takes the ball from Coach Zo. He's ready for his warm-up pitches, but . . . what's this? Ashwell waves the batter back to his spot at the dish and shouts at him. "Get in there, brother. I don't need no warm-ups for you!"

Fine, you could say, didn't take that too kindly. Most everyone else in the stadium got a good chuckle, but Fine looks angry. He bites his lip. He squints his eyes. He has a grip so tight on the bat that he looks like he might melt it. Ashwell gets the sign from DiNuzzio. He shakes him off. He gets another sign. He shakes him off. This is strange because Ashwell only has two pitches. He shakes off his catcher a third time. And a fourth. This must be some sort of psychological game he's playing, trying to rile Fine up. I'd say it's working. He looks like he doesn't just want to hit the ball, but he wants to kill the pitcher.

Finally Ashwell gets a sign he likes. He ever so slowly rocks into his windup. And here's the pitch. . . . Strike right down the middle! Fine didn't even get his *bat off his shoulder. Ashwell laughs. "Be ready for it this time," he says. "Fastball coming through." Again with the mind games. Fine doesn't know what to think. Is Ashwell setting him up or telling the truth?*

Here's the windup, and the pitch. . . . And he was telling the truth! It's a fastball, but it's a good two feet outside. DiNuzzio has to dive to block it, and oh, what a catch! He saved a run there. Heck of a block by Newts. Ashwell laughs again. He brushes the hair out of his eyes and looks back in for the sign.

He winds up, and the pitch . . . It's a slow palmball right at the knees. Fine didn't swing again! And again it's a strike. One ball and two strikes. "Ain't you gonna swing?" Ashwell yells to Fine. Fine says nothing. But the look in his eyes says everything. He's going to swing, and hard. He wants nothing more than his second home run of the game—this one would win it.

Ashwell gets the sign. Here's the pitch. . . . It's the slowest pitch I've ever seen. Fine swings way too early and misses! Strike three! What a performance by Hunter Ashwell.

At this point I stopped announcing the game in my head to stand up and cheer. Hunter was cocky, but he was good. No doubt about that. "Take a seat, brother!" he yelled to Fine. Then he turned around to face his fielders. "And you too," he said.

"All of you. Sit down! No need for any of you for these next two. Take your gloves off. Have a seat. Go home and grab a glass of juice. I got this."

The Schwenkfelder fielders looked at each other and shrugged. None of them sat down. Coach Zo was an old-school kind of coach. He didn't like showboating. I was surprised he let Hunter get away with it. I guess there are rules, and then there are rules for superstars. Hunter was on his way to greatness. Coach Zo really wanted to win this game; otherwise, he would have pulled Hunter out for sure.

What he did do was walk to the mound. Mike got up from behind the plate to join the conversation, as catchers usually do. But Coach Zo held up his hand. This was going to be a private meeting. Well, as private as a meeting could be on the pitcher's mound of a crowded middle school baseball field. Coach Zo leaned in and quietly said something to Hunter. Hunter nodded and didn't say another word. Coach Zo returned to the dugout and Hunter stepped on the rubber. He wasn't done with theatrics, though. He started having a loud conversation with the baseball. "Oh, what's that? You want to go see your friend the glove. Well, all right. Strap in for the ride." Then he threw three straight strikes and started cracking up. Coach Zo didn't look pleased.

Highland was down to its final out. The bases-loaded, nobody-out rally had turned into a desperate last chance. I felt bad for the Highland hitter. It was a little guy. I didn't know his name. Seemed nobody did. I didn't hear fans or even his teammates chanting his name. Maybe they had no hope.

Highland is down to their last out. A mysterious little man with an odd batting stance steps to the dish. He stands like a duck up there, toes pointed in and bat way up in the air. Ashwell gets the sign. He fires a fastball and . . . the batter is late by a long shot. He didn't even start his swing until after the ball hit the glove. That's strike one.

Ashwell is wasting no time. Working quickly now. He gets the sign and lobs a slow one up there, which bounces in the dirt. The batter swings anyway! He misses by a mile. That's strike two. A collective groan goes up from the crowd. Highland is down to its last strike. Ashwell smiles. He nods his head. He kicks his leg. He throws a heater chest-high, right down the middle, strike three. How about that?!

Mike didn't charge out and hug Hunter this time, but he did hop up excitedly. He ran out to the mound and gave a high five.

I heard Hunter yell, "Somebody throw that ball in a bucket of water before it starts shooting sparks. Yee-hah!"

Coach Zo shook his head again. Everyone else laughed.

The team was two and zero. Undefeated. First place. In two games Hunter got a win and a save. His ERA was 0.00 and he had struck out nine batters in a row. If there was ever a more dominant performance in the history of middle school baseball, I couldn't think of it. Maybe it was the greatest pitching performance in the history of baseball.

I thought about Orel Hershiser, who pitched, like, sixty scoreless innings for the Dodgers. And Don Drysdale, who threw six shutouts in a row. Then there was Johnny Vander Meer, who everyone still mentioned all the time because he threw two no-hitters in a row back in the 1930s. Would Hunter Ashwell's name someday be like theirs? A famous pitcher known the world over? Would there be Hunter Ashwell baseball cards? Bobbleheads? Would he be in the Hall of Fame and I'd tell my grandkids, "I knew him when . . ."?

It sure seemed like that this day. He was a star, and the team was riding high.

CHAPTER FOURTEEN

The next game was the following Tuesday. It was an away game against Griffith. I wanted to go. The Schwenkfelder Mustangs were playing the best baseball in the state of Pennsylvania. Better than my beloved Phillies, that's for sure. The Phillies were getting crushed by the Mets. This was bad enough, as Phillies fans and Mets fans pretty much hate each other. But in the Norbeck house it was even worse. Dad had recently revealed his terrible true identity as a Mets fan. He had kept it hidden for years and was apparently making up for lost time by taunting me every chance he got.

"Hey, son," he'd say, first thing in the morning. "Check the standings lately?" That was literally the *first* thing I had to wake up to in the morning. Dad's smug face, peeking out over the sports section of the newspaper.

"Listen, Dad," I'd say. "I'm glad you're happy—"

"I am," he'd say, interrupting me.

"I'm glad you're happy now that your awful secret is out in the open," I'd continue. "But if you want to go back to pretending that you don't care about baseball, that would be great with me."

"Or," he'd say with a stupid smile, "if you want to switch allegiances and join me over here in winner territory, that would be great too. I have a Mets cap in the closet just your size."

"I'd rather put a live porcupine down my pants," I'd say, matching his cheery tone.

"Okay, have a great day at school!" he'd say.

Then he'd start chanting "Let's! Go! Mets!" while I tried to drown him out with "Shut! Up! Dad!" Good times.

All day at school on Tuesday, people were talking about the game. Like I said, baseball was a pretty big deal at Schwenkfelder Middle School. It was a small league, but the stakes were high. If you were a star at SMS, you'd more than likely get a shot at the high school team. And then from there? The whole world opened up to you.

And on this Tuesday, baseball was on the minds of the citizens of SMS even more than usual. The reason for the excitement? Truck Durkin. What, you ask? Truck Durkin? Yes, Truck Durkin.

Truck Durkin was a local legend. His legend in fact stretched beyond the local. Truck Durkin was famous in Philadelphia. Truck Durkin might have been famous throughout the whole world. But the weird thing is, no one knew what he looked like.

Truck Durkin was old, everyone knew that. He had been a baseball scout for at least fifty years, everyone knew that. How old was he when he started? Twenty? Thirty? Forty? It hardly matters. Anything plus fifty equals old. He got his start in scouting after his own playing career ended, when-ever that was. He had an ability to look at a kid and immediately know what his future would be as a ballplayer. Truck Durkin could see a five-year-old hitting off a tee and say, "That kid will hit three hundred in the majors with excellent opposite-field power someday." Truck Durkin could walk by a baby in a crib kicking his legs and say, "That baby will steal fifty bases someday. Look at them legs."

And he'd be right.

Everyone knows the story of Mike Schmidt. Mike Schmidt was the greatest Phillie of all time. He might have been the greatest third baseman *ever* to put on a glove. I say he definitely was. (My dad would say David Wright, but that's just one way you know my father is not a very serious human being.)

But did you know this about Mike Schmidt? He was a terrible baseball player in high school. His batting average was under two hundred! That's one hit every five times at bat. That's, like, really bad for anyone. Terrible for high school. There is, like, zero chance that if you hit under two hundred in high school you'd make the major leagues. Zero chance! That would be like *me* ending up making the majors. And not just making the majors but being an all-star. One of the best third basemen of all time! Okay, maybe it's not quite as unlikely as *me* doing those things, as I hit well under two hundred. I hit about zero hundred. Can you hit a negative number? Lenny Norbeck can.

My point is this: Mike Schmidt was not a very good hitter in high school. Plus, he had two bad knees. But somehow, Truck knew. He just knew. He guessed that Schmidt would make it big, and boy, did he ever. Truck was a direct line to the big time. And he liked to start guys young. So if he was interested in you, it was a very big deal. And rumor had it that warm Tuesday morning at Schwenkfelder Middle School, Truck Durkin was very interested in Hunter Ashwell.

Hunter laughed it off. Took it in stride. Joked about it. "Hey, of course he's interested in the Great Imperial Ashwell. Who isn't?" Maybe he was nervous, but he didn't show it. It takes a special kind of person to be a pitcher. You have to stand there, raised up on the middle of the field, with everyone watching you. You have to want the ball, even after you mess up. You have to believe in yourself with an intensity that bordered on insanity. I mean, you didn't have to be a cocky maniac like Hunter Ashwell, but it didn't hurt either.

Mike, Other Mike, and I discussed Truck over lunch. Other Mike, of course, knew nothing about Truck's legend or even about Mike Schmidt. He did enjoy the conversation, though, mainly because he got a kick out of saying "Truck Durkin" over and over again. It *is* kind of fun to say.

"Truck Durkin, Truck Durkin, Truck Durkin."

"Dude, Other Mike, shut up," Mike said.

I laughed, and added, "Truck Durkin."

"The weird thing about him," Mike said, "is that no one ever sees him coming. That's what my dad said anyway. He said that back when Truck was scouting Schmidt, he didn't want anybody to know.

He wanted to make sure that the Phillies got him, so he'd pretend he wasn't interested. He'd do stuff like lurk in bushes or hide in his station wagon. One time he supposedly watched a game with binoculars from a nearby rooftop."

"Seems pretty shady," Other Mike said. "I don't know if we can trust this Truck Durkin."

"Oh, we can trust him," I said. "He has a reputation for being the best. But if he's always so secretive, why do we all know that he's coming?"

"This is a good point," Mike said, taking a sip of his milk. "Maybe he's getting sloppy in his old age."

"Or maybe Hunter just made up the whole thing to make himself seem awesome."

"That does sound like something Hunter would do," Mike agreed.

"Wow," I said, pretending to be surprised. "Selling out your own battery-mate. Aren't you supposed to defend him?"

"Hey," Mike said. "I just catch him. Don't hold me responsible for the crazy stuff that comes out of his mouth."

"Well, I'll help you guys find out if this Truck Durkin is there or not," Other Mike said. "Wouldn't he have to be ancient?"

"Yeah," we said.

"Well," Other Mike said. "Can't be too hard to find a hundred-year-old guy climbing a tree with a pair of binoculars and a clipboard."

He had a point.

CHAPTER FIFTEEN

Mike was taking the bus with the team, so me and Other Mike made plans to ride our bikes over to Griffith's field. We took the bus home from school, each grabbed our bikes, then met at his house.

"Ready, 'Truck'?" I said. We had a running joke about pretending to be a biker gang with cool and tough nicknames. I thought he'd get a kick out of being called "Truck." I was right. He snorted and a bubble of snot bloomed from his nose. "Sick!" I said. He laughed again.

"Ready, 'Truck,'" he said as we pushed off on our bikes, heading across town.

"We can't both be named 'Truck'!" I said.

"Sure we can," Other Mike said. "I'm Truck, you're Truck. Truck Durkin is Truck. We're all Trucks."

Other Mike was pretty weird sometimes, but hilarious.

The bike ride over to Griffith was fun. I totally won at the end, outsprinting Other Mike as always. We found a bike rack to lock our bikes up and headed over to the field. The players were done warming up and the game would be starting soon.

The first thing I noticed was that they had an announcer's booth too! I was kind of annoyed. It was high up, located behind home plate. It made my own little shack seem shabby by comparison, not that I was complaining.

"What the heck?" I said to Other Mike. "I thought we were the only ones who had a cool announcer's booth."

"Where do you think Mike's dad got the idea?" Other Mike said.

"Well, that stinks," I said.

"Not really. I'm sure you're way better than that guy." He pointed up to the booth and we could see the announcer through the glass. He didn't look like much—a short kid with glasses and a buzz cut. Then, to our surprise, he turned on the microphone.

"Ladies and gentlemen, please rise for the national anthem," he said. His voice was okay. Not better than mine or anything. Then he started to sing. No prerecorded music, nothing. Just this kid, belting it out. And, man, he could *belt* it out. By the time he got to "home of the brave," I felt like I had tears in my eyes. I think everyone in attendance felt the same way. It was a medium-sized crowd. It wasn't big like the Schwenkfelder home crowds, but it was an okay turnout. Lots of parents, including Mike's mom and dad, and other kids. Yet it was totally quiet. Man, that kid was good.

"Jeez," I whispered to Other Mike. "Way to make me look bad, kid."

"You're still the best," he said.

The whole crowd stayed quiet. And then there was a recognizable squeak over the loudspeaker. Well, it was recognizable to me. It was the noise that the microphone made when you bumped into it or dropped it or something. I looked up at the booth. There, joining the short guy with the amazing singing voice, was someone in a Schwenkfelder uniform! I saw the maroon hat and jersey, but I couldn't tell who it was. The microphone clicked.

"Ladies and gentlemen," he said. "This is the Great Imperial Ashwell speaking." I looked over to the Schwenkfelder dugout and saw Coach Zo shaking his head. He was also turning bright red and his eyes were bugging out of his skull. "I see an enormous number of you have come today to see the Great Imperial Ashwell pitch. How would you like to have me go to the mound and strike out every batter I face?"

If he was expecting applause, he didn't get it. A few people from the Griffith side booed. A few people laughed. Mostly people looked uncomfortable. Even Hunter's own team looked embarrassed. I couldn't tell what Mike was thinking because he had pulled his catcher's mask on. I imagined that he was rolling his eyes.

"What was that?" Other Mike said. "*Great Imperial Ashwell?* Sounds awesome."

"Yeah," I said. "But it's really rude to be so cocky, don't you think?"

"I guess," Other Mike said. "But I have a job to do."

"Good luck looking for Truck, Truck," I said.

"Got it, Truck," he said.

Other Mike really was a good friend. He was braver than people gave him credit for. And cooler than people gave him credit for. Basically, people didn't give him credit for anything, but he ruled. "You rule, Other Mike," I said. He nodded.

And with that, he was off. He started walking

really slowly, taking huge steps like he was sneaking up on someone. I rolled my eyes and laughed.

Hunter continued on with his pregame rant. "I'm going to take my time. I have a few things to say and they can't start the game without me. It's funny what a few no-hitters can do for a man. They make you feel *goood*. So good I think I'm going to throw another one here tonight! I'm about to debut a pitch never seen by this generation, or any generation. So please, ladies and gentlemen, enjoy."

We were the visiting team, so that meant we batted first. Turned out they could start the game without Hunter. The home team took the field. Byron Lucas was hitting leadoff and was all ready to step into the batter's box. But he was waiting for the go-ahead from Coach Zo, and Coach Zo was nowhere to be seen. I searched the field and found him—of all places—on Griffith's bench. Well, he wasn't sitting on the bench, he was leaning up against it, deep in conversation with Coach Fenner of the Griffins. Coach Moyer looked around. The umpire walked over there, apparently to ask if there was a problem. Coach Zo held up a finger like "just a moment," then finished his conversation.

What was that about? Was Coach Fenner mad because of Hunter? It was hard to read his face. He was one of those guys who always looked mad, like Mr. Webb.

Coach Zo strode back across the field, his hands in his pockets. He never looked mad. He looked as calm and cool as always. Finally, the coaches were in their spots. The pitcher was on the mound. Hunter was back in the dugout. The umpire yelled, "Play ball!" Then he threw the ball to the Griffith pitcher, who I recognized as Jagdish Sheth. If Jagdish was upset by Hunter's antics, he didn't show it. He just pulled his hat low over his eyes and started to pitch.

I began announcing in my head.

Jagdish Sheth takes the hill for the Griffith Griffins. They're looking for revenge after being blanked in the historic perfect game to open the season against their visitors today, the Schwenkfelder Mustangs. Sheth is not a big guy, but he has a decent fastball and good control. We've already had some theatrics today, as Hunter Ashwell pulled the unprecedented stunt of announcing his greatness into the microphone before the first pitch was thrown. Should be an interesting one. . . .

The top half of the first wasn't that interesting, though. Not really. Our guys managed a hit and a walk against Jagdish, but Nathan Gub lined into a double play and the inning was over. The sides changed and Schwenkfelder headed onto the field. Mike took his customary spot behind the plate and Hunter fired a few warm-up tosses. I thought about his line the other day: "Get in there, brother. I don't need no warm-ups for you!" Man, that must be really annoying if you're on the other team. Especially because he could back it up.

Hunter's pitches looked sharp in warm-ups. He fired one pitch over the inside corner, then another over the outside corner. He mixed the fast ones with the slow ones. He was ready.

The first batter stepped up to the plate and knocked the dirt out of his cleats with his bat. I almost felt bad for him. The odds of getting a hit are never that good, really. Even the best hitter fails to get a hit two out of every three times. And if you were facing a guy who pitched a perfect game against you only a week ago? Let's just say that the Griffith Griffins could not have been feeling very positive about their chances.

But yet, as that first batter stepped into the batter's box, I noticed something odd. He wasn't cowering. He wasn't nervous. He wasn't upset. He had a definite glimmer in his eye, a definite hop to his step. And, unless I was mistaken, he was smiling.

I started to announce in my head.

The Schwenkfelder pitcher Hunter Ashwell is a little man with a big mouth and a bigger right arm. He's been talking an even bigger game than usual today, but not without reason. He threw a perfect game against Griffith last time and claims he'll do the same today. His warm-ups are sharp and he looks ready to roll.

Newts gives the sign. Ashwell nods. He rocks into his windup. Here's the pitch and . . . Well, the perfect game is over. Johnny Vander Meer, your record is safe. There will be no back-to-back no-hitters here. That ball is gone, long gone over the scoreboard in center field. Hunter Ashwell looks shocked, absolutely shocked. He literally cannot believe what just happened. The first pitch of the game is a home run and a one-to-nothing lead for the Griffith Griffins.

Mike did a good job as catcher and went out to the mound to calm Hunter down. It didn't seem to work, but that wasn't Mike's fault. He did what a catcher is supposed to do. Tell the pitcher to forget about it, get the next guy. Mike went back to his crouch behind the plate. The umpire threw Hunter a new ball. He caught it in his glove and stared at it like he didn't even know what it was. Like some strange animal had fallen from the sky and taken up residence in his baseball mitt.

"You'll get this guy," I yelled from my spot in the stands, trying to offer some encouragement.

I was wrong.

Hunter didn't get the next guy. Or the next guy. Or the guy after that. The first four hitters absolutely smashed the ball. They hit line drives all over the place. Two more runs scored. It was unbelievable! The score was three to nothing before the first out was even recorded. Both Robert and Trebor Fenner had hits. The fifth batter up, a lefty, hit a hard line drive too. But he hit it right at Kyle Webb, who caught it and stepped on first for a double play. Hunter sighed and settled down to get the sixth batter on a groundout. But it was hit hard. Everything was.

Schwenkfelder scratched out a run in the top of the second, but Griffith came right back swinging. They smacked line drive after line drive, one more of which went for a home run. The score was nine to one here in the bottom of the second inning. Griffith was going to win by the run rule if this kept up. The whoop rule going *against* us! With Hunter Ashwell on the mound! It was simply unbelievable.

Coach Zo had apparently seen enough. He went out to the mound to tell Hunter to hit the showers. A very surprised Noah Stewart was given the call to the mound. Noah wasn't a bad player, but he was *maybe* the fifth-best pitcher on the team. There was no way he thought he'd get into a game Hunter was starting. But there he was, on the mound, trying to salvage one for Schwenkfelder.

While Noah warmed up, Other Mike came back over and sat next to me on the bleachers.

"So what did you find?" I asked. "Any sign of the great Truck Durkin?"

"Not that I could see," Other Mike said. "And I looked everywhere. Up trees, around the fence. I checked every single car. I don't think he's spying from a nearby building."

"Good deduction," I said. "Given that there are no nearby buildings."

"Right," Other Mike said. It was true. The only building nearby was the school, and it was pretty far away and not really tall enough to get an angle on the field from. "And my helper couldn't find any signs of Truck either," he added.

"Your helper?" I said. Other Mike pointed over toward the concession stands. Even from the backs of their heads I could recognize who was in line.

"Davis Gannett?" I said. "What is he doing here?"

"He likes to watch baseball games, I guess," Other Mike said. "I agree with you, it's a terribly strange way for a person to entertain themselves. But I suppose there is no accounting for taste." He flashed that big, goofy Other Mike–ian smile.

"Very funny," I said. "Don't you think it's weird that he keeps showing up? It's like he's stalking the team. It's . . . creepy."

"Yeah, Len," Other Mike said. "Nothing ironic about *you* saying that."

"Well, it's different with me," I said.

"Different how?"

"He got kicked off the team!"

"You were never on the team!"

"I'm the announcer!"

"Are you announcing today?"

"Just shut up, Other Mike," I said. "And go back to looking for Truck."

"He ain't here," Other Mike said. "I told you. Me and Davis looked everywhere."

"Probably a good thing," I said. "Did you see how Hunter got destroyed out there?"

"No," Other Mike said. "I did not."

Noah did okay as the new pitcher. He limited the damage. Schwenkfelder scored a few more runs, so the run rule wasn't put into effect. Still, we were too far behind to come back. The final score was twelve to five, Griffith. Hunter's stats for the day were the exact opposite of his first start. He had gone just one and one-third innings. He had given up nine runs on twelve hits. If he hadn't lucked out on that double play, things could have been much, much worse.

A tough one here in Griffith, sports fans. Sometimes you're perfect, sometimes you're far from it. . . .

After the game, I went over to chat with Mike. Some of the guys were taking the bus back to school, but because his parents were there, he was going straight home with them. There was no celebratory pizza this day. We stood in the grass next to the field, leaning against the chain-link fence.

"Tough one," I said.

"You got that right," Mike said. His face was streaked with dirt and his hair was slick with sweat.

He was sipping on a cup of water. He looked like he had been through a war. "I just don't get it. How do you go from being perfect to being perfectly terrible?"

"Just a rough outing," I said.

"You think?" Mike said.

"Sure," I said. "Happens to everyone. Happens to the best pitchers in the world. Even could happen to the Great Imperial Ashwell."

"Can you believe that stunt with the microphone?" Mike asked. "I thought Coach Zo was going to kill him."

"I'm surprised he didn't bench him," I said.

"Me too," Mike said. "I guess the rules are different for the great ones."

"Or the formerly great ones," I said. "Just kidding. He'll get it back. You'll get them next time. Just an unlucky break."

Davis Gannett butted into the conversation. "Hey, you dork-buckets," he said. "Sorry to interrupt."

"No you're not," Mike said.

"Well, listen," Davis spat. "Ain't no way the massacre we just witnessed had anything to do with luck."

Mike and I kept our mouths shut. We just stared at each other, then looked back at Davis.

"You think luck is going to turn a bunch of weak-hitting dork-buckets like the Griffith Griffins into a whole team of Babe Ruths? Luck has nothing to do with it."

"What, then?" I said. "You can't really blame Hunter. He's been nothing but great all year."

Davis sneered. "Yeah, the Great Imperial Ashwell has been great. He *is* great. But if and only if they don't know what's coming."

"What are you saying?" Mike asked.

"That he ain't good if they do know what is coming! Do I have to spell it out for you?"

"You know how to spell?" I said. It was mean.

Davis got right in my face. "You shut up, Lenny. I know a lot of things. And one thing I know for certain: Griffith was stealing your friend's signs."

"No way!" Mike said. "We have a secret system!"

"Well, the secret's out," Davis said. "You stink."

For a moment I thought Mike was going to take a swing at Davis. But Coach Zo walked up and yelled, "Let's go! Team meeting, pronto!"

I didn't know what *pronto* meant, but you could

tell by the way he said it that he was *not* joking around.

Other Mike and I got onto our bikes. I didn't have the heart to make up wacky nicknames. I just glumly snapped on the helmet and started to pedal.

"Hey," I said as we rode. "Where was Davis when you ran into him?"

"Here," Other Mike said. "At the game."

"No," I said. "Where *exactly* was he?"

"Out by the fence," he said. "Way out there." He pointed toward center field.

"What was he doing out there?" I asked.

Other Mike shrugged. "He said he didn't like sitting where everyone could see him. Said everyone kept giving him mean looks. I think he's right. You and Mike are both pretty mean to him. I'm not sure why."

"You're not sure why?!" I yelled. "He's been mean to *us* our whole lives!"

"Well, he's different now," Other Mike said, though Davis's behavior just a few minutes ago was evidence to the contrary. "I thought you'd think it was a good thing that he was here to support the team or whatever."

"Yeah," I scoffed. "Support the team. Ha."

CHAPTER SIXTEEN

That night, Mike called me. He wasn't known for calling very much, so I could tell something was wrong.

"Hey, Newts," I said.

"Hey, Len," he said.

"Tough loss," I said.

"Yeah," he said. "Knocks us out of first place."

"Aren't you tied, though?"

"I guess," he said. "But we're almost in last."

"Don't feel too bad," I said. "It's easy to fall from first place to last when there are only three teams in the league. Even last is only third. Hey, could you be tied for third? You'd be in first and last at the same time! Wait, I'm not sure—"

"Stop making fun of our league," he said.

"Not making fun!"

There was a pause.

"So do you think there is any chance that Davis is right?" he asked.

"No," I said. "You are definitely not a dork-bucket."

"Not that! Do you think that someone is stealing our . . . stealing our signs?" He sounded like a little kid caught with his hand in the cookie jar. He sounded ashamed. He sounded guilty.

"Well," I said, trying to remain upbeat. "It's certainly possible. I mean, don't take it the wrong way or anything. It happens to lots of guys. Big-league catchers have it happen to them all the time. Remember how Pap was just talking about it in that interview the other day?"

Davey Pappenheimer was the Phillies manager. He was a little eccentric—which, according to my dad, is just a way of saying a rich person is crazy. I don't know if Pap is crazy, but he *is* pretty entertaining. Sample Pap quote: "Yeah, there's more than one way to skin a cat. In fact, there's six. And I've done all six. One I'll never do again and I don't recommend it and I'll thank you never to bring it up again." This was in a discussion regarding the hit-and-run.

I continued. "Pap was saying that the Mets are stealing signs from your boy Famosa. And you know he's a crafty catcher. If the stupid Mets could steal signs from someone as crafty as Ramon Famosa, it could happen to anyone."

"But we have a system!" he said. "Hunter and I worked with Coach Zo to make a secret system. It's the most secret system of all secret systems."

"As you have mentioned," I said. He seriously has mentioned it about a million times.

"I won't even tell you, and you're my best friend!"

"Thanks," I said. It was nice to hear. I kind of did wish he would tell me their system, but I wasn't going to push it.

It was silent for a minute. Neither of us knew what to say.

"I'll take the case," I said.

"What?"

"The case," I said. "I'll take the case. The case of the stolen signs. Lenny Norbeck: baseball announcer, detective, solid B student. You know, I have a pretty impressive résumé for a middle schooler."

"Don't forget to add dork-bucket to the list," Mike said with a laugh.

I laughed too.

"You really think someone is stealing the signs?"

"They have to be," I said. "Now that I think about it, there's no way Hunter all of a sudden became so hittable. It's like night and day."

"It can't be that Griffith suddenly has him figured out," he said. "They're, like, the worst team in the league."

"Third place isn't that bad," I joked.

"Out of three it is," he said. We laughed. "So you think you can crack the case *while* announcing ball games?"

"I can crack the case while announcing ball games, whistling 'Dixie,' drinking a quart of milk, and farting the national anthem."

"Just do the first two, okay?"

"Okay."

I knew what my plan for the next day would be: a trip to the library.

CHAPTER SEVENTEEN

I took the bus home from school, chucked my backpack into my room, had a quick snack, and got out my bike. I snapped on the helmet, ready to ride alone to the library. There was no game scheduled that day. There was practice, so Mike was busy. I called Other Mike up, but he was hanging out with Davis! Ridiculous. I had no desire to join that team. Oh yeah, I guess I probably had some home-work. But I didn't feel like doing it.

I decided to put my brainpower to better use. Was someone from Griffith stealing Mike's signs? How were they doing it? Baseball announcers are always saying that there is nothing new under the sun, so I figured I'd learn a little about the history of sign stealing in baseball.

The afternoon was warm and the ride was nice enough. I passed the huge Schwenkfelder Church, its spire trying to touch the sky and its bright stained-glass windows twinkling in reds and yellows. I passed the Schwenkfelder Cemetery, thinking sad thoughts about all the people buried there. I took it slow, turning down a side road next to a farm so I could wave hello to the cows like I did when I was little. I think I really used to think that they'd be sad if I didn't say hello. I was a weird kid. Maybe all kids were weird kids. . . .

Eventually the boxy red building that is the Schwenkfelder Library was visible up the road. I decided to pedal as fast as I could, though of course I had no one to race against. I announced out loud this dramatic sprint, finishing with a frenzied "OH MY GOD, HE HAS DONE IT AGAIN, LENNY NORBECK HAS WON THE TOUR DE SCHWENKFELDER FOR AN UNPRECEDENTED ELEVENTH TIME IN TEN YEARS. WHAT THE I DON'T EVEN? HOW IS THAT EVEN POSSIBLE?!"

An old lady leaving the library with a green canvas bag loaded with books gave me a weird look as she walked to her car. I nodded and said, "Tour de Schwenkfelder. You know how it is. You know how I do." She apparently did not. Some people were never young, I guess.

I locked up my bike, took off my helmet, and carried it into the library. Schwenkfelder is lucky to have a great librarian, the portly Mr. Bonzer. Sure, for a while I thought he was the evil blogger PhilzFan1 and possibly a murderer, but that was just a misunderstanding. I was happy to see him at his usual spot, his large rump filling up the chair behind the reference desk.

"Leonard Norbeck," he said before I even had a chance to say hello. "Where are the Mikes?"

"Long story," I said. "I'm flying solo today."

"Cool beans," he said, which is the kind of epically dorky thing only a librarian would say. Come to think of it, "flying solo" is a pretty dorky thing to say. Shut up.

"Looking for anything in particular? Doing some homework?"

"Um, what?" I said.

"You know: homework? It's schoolwork, only you do it at home. Stop me if you've heard of it." He shifted in his seat and let out a huge sigh.

"Oh yeah, that," I said. "No, I'm not here doing homework."

"Color me shocked," he replied, holding a hand to his mouth in mock surprise. Then he smiled his classic gap-toothed Bonzer smile.

"What I'm actually wondering about is . . . how to steal signs in a baseball game."

Mr. Bonzer now gave me that other classic Bonzer expression: the skeptical eyebrow raise. He paused for a long moment, then pushed himself up from his chair, slowly rising to his feet like an elephant lumbering from a nap.

"Lenny," he said. "It is my solemn duty as an information retrieval specialist to help honor any request for information without passing judgment, but I'm going to feel really bad about myself if I'm helping you help the Schwenkfelder Middle School baseball team cheat."

"What? No!" I said. "It's not that at all. I think the other team is cheating. I'm trying to figure out how to *catch* them."

"Good," he said. "Now I will sleep better at night. Actually, I always sleep well. Like a beautiful baby."

"Hey, so do you really have to answer any question anyone asks?" I said. "Like if they ask how to make a bomb or the best way to make someone pee their pajamas during a sleepover?"

"Put their hand in a bowl of warm water while they sleep. Well, duh. Easy."

"Thanks," I said. We were getting sort of off

track. He walked over to one of the computers you use to look up books and quickly tapped out his search. He looked puzzled, then confused, then determined, then happy.

"So, as it happens, we do have a book on the subject that you are looking for. It is called *The Semilegal Guide to Cheating at Baseball* and it seems like it will be a good read." He scribbled down the Dewey decimal number and we walked to the book's home on the shelves. I almost got distracted looking around at all the other baseball books that surrounded it, but I forced myself to stay focused. Mr. Bonzer pulled the book off the shelf and handed it to me. It was a slim volume that looked like it had been around for a long time.

"Thanks!" I said. Then I added, "Hey, is there any way to tell if this book has been checked out recently?"

"I can't tell you that type of thing," he said. "Librarians' honor. We have strict privacy laws."

"As you mentioned," I said. "But I'm not asking *who* checked it out. Just *if* it was checked out."

"You know," he said, "if your career as a detective doesn't work out, you should consider becoming a lawyer. You're truly good at always finding the technicalities."

"That's why they call me 'the Human Technicality,'" I said. "Go ahead. You can call me that."

"Still looking for that perfect nickname, huh?" he said. "I suggest that you keep looking."

"Yeah," I said. "You got a point."

"Give me a minute," he said. "I'll go look up the last time the book was checked out. Shouldn't be hard to tell."

He slowly made his way back toward his desk, muttering something about "the Human Technicality." It *was* a catchy nickname! While he walked, I flipped the book open and began skimming the pages. It seemed like people had cheated at baseball in just about every way a person could imagine. There were all sorts of ways to make a ball do unnatural things. Besides good old spit, pitchers had also used licorice, mud, wax, or even a bit of soap. I guess soap was good because if you got caught with it on you, you could just claim to be a neat freak.

One team even used a potato. The way that worked was that the catcher would keep a potato in his pocket. He'd wait until a runner was on third. He'd catch the pitch, then pretend to be trying to pick the runner off third. He'd fire the potato over the third baseman's head, and the runner would trot home, thinking he'd score an easy run. Only there waiting would be the catcher, ball in hand. He'd apply the tag and the runner would be shocked. (Note: You'd probably want to warn your third baseman.)

Mr. Bonzer slowly made his way back toward me. I must have been zoning out because he was like, "Ahem—interesting, I take it?"

I showed the paragraph to Mr. Bonzer about potatoes. He read and smiled.

"Nothing specific in the rulebooks against chucking vegetables, I guess," I said.

"Technically, the potato is a tuber," he said.

"Yeah, whatever." I made a mental note to tell Mike about the potato trick, in case his team could use it somewhere down the line. It didn't seem exactly legal, but one never knows when one has to resort to unconventional means to win a ball game. Or catch a criminal.

"So," I said, hoping for my first break in the case. "Has this been checked out recently?"

"Yes, sir," he said. "In fact, it just came back yesterday. Funny, a lot of the old books like this sit here on these dusty shelves for years, but this one has been getting a workout, I guess."

"Oh, it's funny all right," I said. "Ha-ha-freaking-ha."

Bonzer gave me a weird look. "Anything else I can do for you?"

"You sure you can't tell me who had the book out?" I asked. "I won't tell anyone you told. Totally our little secret."

"Afraid I can't do that, Lenny," he said, putting on a weird accent for some reason. I think he was pretending to be a guy in a Mob movie. You know, like an old-fashioned Italian gangster. "Afraid I can't do that, Lenny." He said it again, cracking himself up so hard he had to put a hand on the bookshelves to keep from falling over. The shelves almost toppled over under his weight. Then he composed himself and said, "Seriously, no. There is zero chance. We don't even keep those records."

"Pretty hush-hush," I said. "Kinda weird." He shrugged. Then I went back to flipping through the book. "Can you tell me about this?" I showed him the chapter entitled "The Shot Heard Round the World"—about a famous home run in 1951 that might have benefited from sign stealing. "Were you at that game?"

"Lenny," he said. "I was born in 1975."

"Oh," I said.

"I do know the basic story, though," he said. "Bobby Thomson hit the shot off Ralph Branca to win the series. Years later there was some speculation that he had help. Maybe even proof that someone gave Thomson the signs."

While he was talking, I kept reading. People don't usually love that, but I didn't think a librarian would mind. "Yeah, yeah, they used a telescope," I said. "Some guy named Hank Schenz used a telescope from center field to see the catcher's fingers. Then he'd press a button to buzz in the bullpen. The guys there flashed the sign to the batter. Genius."

"Think about how much easier it would be these days," Bonzer said. "With Bluetooth, that sort of thing."

"Bluetooth the pirate?" I said.

"Blue*beard* was the pirate," he said. "Bluetooth is a wireless phone thing. I mean, you know, with laptops and smartphones, all that kind of stuff. Wouldn't it be pretty easy to communicate secretly during a game?"

"You read my mind," I said. "You read my mind."

He nodded seriously at me and tapped his nose with his finger. Weird guy.

I flipped through the book a little more. There

was a story about the Brewers using a telescope to steal signs and having the mascot wave a signal. A few others with similar tales—guys using telescopes or binoculars to see the catcher's sign and then flashing a signal to the batter. Then I got distracted by a story from the really old days of baseball. Apparently, John McGraw, who was a third baseman before he became a famous manager, would hook his fingers in base runners' belts. So if you were on third and trying to tag up, he'd just grab you by the belt and you'd be stuck. Once, to counter this, a runner loosened his belt. McGraw yanked the belt clean off. The guy's pants fell around his ankles, but he scored the winning run. He totally taunted McGraw in his undies. Like I said, sometimes a man has to do what a man has to do.

Bonzer was still standing there. "So you think that someone is stealing Schwenkfelder's signs, huh?" he asked.

"Yeah," I said. I told him all about the Great Imperial Hunter Ashwell and his amazing performance, then the strange game against Griffith.

Bonzer sighed and rubbed his beard. "Maybe he's tipping pitches," he said. "Maybe they figured out what to look for."

"I don't think so," I said. "Mike says Coach Zo filmed Hunter pitching. He slowed the footage down. Watched it backward and forward. It's next to impossible to tell if he's throwing the fast one or the Long, Slow Sally. That's what he calls it."

Mr. Bonzer laughed. "This Hunter sounds like a real character."

"Yeah," I said. "He's kind of a jerk. But he's a great pitcher. And my friend Mike is the catcher."

"Oh, right," Bonzer said. "That's why you're in here. Trying to help Mike. You're a good friend, Lenny."

"I try to be," I said guiltily. I didn't mention how many times I secretly hoped Mike wouldn't make the team. How jealous I was of him. I felt like a terrible person for that. And how I thought that maybe he only was Hunter's catcher because he got Davis Gannett busted for stealing a cell phone he never stole! There! I said it! It feels good to get it out.

But helping him was the right thing to do, so I resolved to keep trying.

"Can I check this book out?" I said.

"Do you have your library card?" he asked.

"You know that I do not," I said. "I'm notorious

for losing library cards. I've lost, like, twelve, which averages out to about two a year since kinder-garten."

"I believe it's more like five a year," he said.

"So you're allowed to keep track of how many library cards I've had, but you can't tell me who checked out this book?" I yelled.

"I can tell you to be quiet," he said. "Those are my solemn duties. Protecting readers' privacy. Shushing loudies. And giving you a hard time for losing your library card."

"Can I have the book anyway?"

"Fine," he said. "But don't tell my boss."

I wanted to yell out "Bonzer told me what other people read and let me borrow this book without my card" just to break all his three rules at once. But then I noticed something fall out of the pages. A small receipt. It didn't have the name of the person who checked out the book last, but it did have the name of another book they borrowed. It was *The Murder of Roger Ackroyd*. This was getting in-teresting.

For once, I kept my mouth shut. I snapped my helmet on and rode off into the sunset.

CHAPTER EIGHTEEN

The sun wasn't really setting. Not quite yet anyway. I rode my bike home at a leisurely pace. This time I wasn't trying to win the Tour de Schwenkfelder. I was trying to get some thinking done. I rode in a winding path, snaking slowly through the quiet streets. I felt just like a detective mulling over a big case. Actually, two cases—only one of which Mike knew about. *Was* someone from Griffith stealing signs? And *was* Davis Gannett innocent in the case of the missing cell phone?

I started taking the long way home and realized I wasn't too far from Griffith Middle School. Schwenkfelder isn't a very big town. Even though I had to cross one or two major streets, it wasn't too hard to get to Griffith. I knew the way. Schwenkfelder is the kind of town that has just about two major streets. Everything is not far off those two.

One of them is called Center Street. It runs through the center of town. I wonder how Sam Schwenk-felder and the other geniuses who formed this town ever thought up that one. Just kidding. There was no Sam Schwenkfelder. Maybe there was. What do I know? I was pretty sure there was a project on local history every year, but I was *quite* sure that I never paid attention.

I rode my bike across Center and into Griffith territory. I started to formulate a plan. I felt like a spy sneaking into enemy turf. Of course no one knew I was from Schwenkfelder Middle. And probably no one would really care. But still, it felt dangerous and exciting.

I realized I wasn't going to see a pair of binoculars hanging on a fence post, but maybe a clue would present itself. The bike ride down Center to Griffith was a lot longer than I remembered it being last time we went that way. Probably because we took a car. Cars make everything seem shorter. But I had all the time in the world, with both Mike and Other Mike busy and the only thing waiting for me at home being homework.

Finally I saw Griffith Middle School. It is a long brick building with about a hundred windows. It actually looks a lot like SMS, which leads me to wonder if all middle schools are designed by the same person. What a weird job that is. They should let middle school students design middle schools. They would be awesome. How hard is it to design a building? I should totally be an architect. You got walls, a floor, some windows. Boom: I'm an architect. Oops, just realized I forgot a roof. Maybe I should stick to announcing.

And to detecting.

I got myself mentally into detective mode as I rode my bike across the parking lot and up the long walkway that went behind the school to the baseball field. I pulled my bike up onto the sidewalk and stood with one foot on the ground and the other on the pedal. I tried to look casual as I scanned the field for hidden spy spots.

The Griffith team was still on the field. I had forgotten that they'd probably have practice. But from the looks of it, the practice was winding down. Most of the players were already headed back toward the school. A few remained on the field, scooping up stray balls and throwing them into a bucket. The coaches were milling around too. I decided I'd wait until they were all gone before I got down to serious sleuthing.

I got my library book out of my backpack and

started flipping through the pages while the practice finished up. Some of the players from Griffith walked past me on the way to the locker room. I kept my head down and the book up over my face. I didn't know if any of them would recognize me from the games at Schwenkfelder, but it was a risk I didn't want to run. Head down, book up, I read. There was a pretty funny section about a player named Eddie Stanky who was part of that famous 1951 home run I was talking about with Bonzer. Stanky was apparently a notoriously mean player. He'd lie, cheat, steal, and do whatever it took to win. I'm no psychologist here, but I'm going to go out on a limb and say that maybe part of the reason he had a chip on his shoulder was that his name was Eddie Stanky. They'd eat him alive in middle school. Stanky. Ha-ha.

After I spent a few minutes reading about Mr. Stanky and the various ways signs have been stolen over the years, the field was empty. Finally, all the Griffith players had gone back to their locker room. They were no doubt hatching future evil schemes. I imagined them cackling like evil villains. "And then we'll use a spy camera! Mwahahaha! And then we'll kidnap their dogs so they can't concentrate on the game! Mwahahaha! And then we'll sell the dogs and use the money for illegal bats and brass knuckles! Mwahahaha." And so on. I had to catch them before this thing got severely out of control, obviously. We can't have the Griffith Griffins out there arming themselves with brass knuckles and stolen dogs. Obviously.

I walked over to the bike rack and chained my bike. I was always careful about bike theft. Even in a town like Schwenkfelder, you can't be too safe. I put my backpack on my back and began walking. Nice and casual. I started scouting out the field. I thought about how *The Semilegal Guide to Cheating at Baseball* said that sign stealing was basically done with variations on the same method. Someone sat in the outfield with binoculars or some way to see the catcher's sign. Then he used a signaling device to quickly show the batter what was coming. The sign stealer would be in the bullpen or the bleachers or hidden in the scoreboard. Every stadium basically had at least one place where an evildoer could perch to do his evil.

I scanned the field. It was obvious. Here, at the Griffith Middle School field, I knew right where I'd start. There was a billboard in center field, an unusual thing for a middle school stadium. And this one was unusual even for a billboard. First of all, it was huge. It stretched across, like, all of right-center field. And second of all, it had a car driving through it. Okay, it wasn't a real car. It was just that the front of the billboard was built out and it was all painted to look like the wood was smashed. How a car was supposed to be driving up in the air through a billboard was beyond me, but that's Griffith for you. Not exactly geniuses.

The billboard said FENNER'S AUTOMOBILES! so I made a mental note never to buy from Fenner's Automobiles. Not that I was in the market for a used car, but you know what I mean. I walked slowly around the field and tried to figure out where a spy might be hiding. I made my way to deep center. I looked up at the back of the billboard. It wasn't a very high fence, but the billboard was enormous—probably about thirty feet tall. And yup, sure enough, there was a ladder going up the back. It wasn't like the ladder was just propped there—it was built into the fence. A ladder wasn't proof of anything. But maybe, I thought, if I climbed it, I could find what I was looking for.

I'm not afraid of heights, not really. Not like Other Mike, who is so afraid of heights that he won't even wear shoes with a heel. He won't even walk on a sheet of paper lying on the floor. He won't even . . . What's thinner than a piece of paper? Nothing, probably. You get my point. But I'm okay with heights. More or less.

I gave the ladder a good shake to make sure it was sturdy. Maybe someone was climbing up and down from there every day to steal signs, but maybe no one had been up there in years. Maybe it was all rusted through and would wait until I was on the top rung before it collapsed. I gave it a solid shake and it didn't collapse. It didn't budge. Perfect for climbing. I took a deep breath, adjusted my backpack, and started to head up.

CHAPTER NINETEEN

I got about three rungs up off the ground when I heard something whiz past my ear! I thought maybe it was a bee, of which I am no fan. But it definitely was no bee. Worse. It was a baseball. It clanged off the metal of the ladder and flew back out into the grass behind the field. What was going on? I spun my head around and another ball flew past, this one barely missing my foot. I had to get down from there! I was like a sitting duck. Man, what a dumb expression. Why is a sitting duck something that can easily get nailed? Can't the stupid duck simply stand up? And seriously, duck, you have wings. Just fly away! I wished I was a duck. Actually, an eagle. Anything with wings! It would have been so awesome to fly out of there.

But I couldn't fly. And I couldn't climb—up or down. Baseballs were coming at me from all directions! All I could do was jump. I pushed off the ladder and leapt backward, tumbling to the ground. My backpack fell off, so I turned to scoop it up. I had no idea where the balls were coming from, so I had no idea which direction to run. Also, it was kind of hard to see because I was trying to cover my face with my hands. More balls were whizzing past me. One hit me in the back. Then another! I had to get out of there.

I took my hands away from my face and started to run. Every time I tried to look around to see who was chucking baseballs at me, another ball flew by. All I could do was keep my head down and keep running. My heart was pounding, my palms were sweating, and I'm not going to lie to you: I was scared. Somehow I sprinted around the field and made it back to my bike without serious injury. I hopped on it and started to pedal away.

Only it was still locked to the bike rack.

I fell off the bike, and my backpack got stuck in the bike rack. My arms were tangled in the straps. This time I felt like not just a sitting duck, but a duck with its feathers plucked and its wings tied to a bike rack. All I could think was *I'm done for*. And I was. First one ninja came toward me, then another. That's right: ninjas! They were both wearing the ninja uniform or whatever you call it, which covered their faces and left just their eyes peering through. Their evil, mean, beady little eyes.

And then they got closer and I realized they weren't ninjas. They were just guys wearing green sweatshirts pulled tight over their faces and tied in the back. Still, it made them impossible to recognize. Well, not impossible. Their ninja costumes both said the same thing across the front: GRIFFITH GRIFFINS BASEBALL.

One of the ninjas approached. I struggled to move but only succeeded in getting myself further tangled up in the bike rack. The ninja laughed, and then so did his friend. They said something to each other in a strange language I couldn't understand. Then they laughed again.

"U-um, guys," I stammered. "Dudes. I don't know who you are or who you think I am, but I assure you I'm not the guy you think—" The second ninja cut me off and raised a hand.

"Well, well, well," he said.

I have found that whenever anyone says "Well, well, well," that's the exact opposite of how things are about to go. It means things were *not* going well. I struggled more mightily.

He laughed. "I think you're pretty well stuck," he said.

He had a strange high-pitched voice and an accent I couldn't place. I thought that maybe he was trying to disguise his voice. Like maybe he didn't want me to be able to identify him. Like maybe the police were going to get involved and he wanted to be able to deny it. I didn't like the sound of that. What did he have in mind?

"Yeah," I said. "Stuck. Maybe you can give me a hand?" Mom always told me to try to make friends, no matter the situation. I don't think she had this in mind, but it was all I could come up with at the moment.

Both ninjas laughed. Their laughs sounded evil. They spoke to each other again in their strange language. I don't speak anything other than English and, like, a tiny bit of Spanish. (*¿Puedo ir al baño?*) I know some Yiddish phrases, but they don't come in all that handy. What I mean is, it didn't even sound like any language I had ever *heard*. Who were these guys?

"I can give you more than a hand," said the first green ninja. He had the same high-pitched voice, the same weird accent. Maybe it wasn't an act.

"Yeah?" I asked. Though, to be honest, I should have seen it coming.

"Yeah," he said. "I can give you a whole fist."

And with that, he punched me in the face.

I don't know what exactly happened after that. I mean, my face hurt, I know that. His fist was small, but he was strong. The punch caught me square in the eye. I didn't know if I should scream for help or cry. What I wanted to do was punch him back, or at least block him before he did it again. But my arms were all twisted up and I was totally stuck. Screaming for help didn't seem like the coolest thing to do, but sometimes you just have to do it.

"Help!" I screamed. "Somebody help me!" There didn't seem to be anyone around, but there had to be coaches or teachers or some grown-up who could swoop in. Nope. None of those. But there was one person who did hear my cries.

"Hey!" the voice yelled. "Stop it!"

At first I didn't recognize the voice. I mean, I recognized it, but I couldn't place it. It was vaguely familiar, like a distant relative you haven't seen for a long time calling you up to wish you a happy birthday. And you're like, "Why are you calling me? How is it a birthday gift to have to spend time in an awkward conversation with you? You know what would have been an even better gift? You *not* calling me. Or maybe just, I don't know, maybe an envelope full of cash?!"

I heard the voice again. "Knock it off, you idiots!" it screamed. And then I heard a *thwack*.

Oh, great, I thought. *Another baseball-throwing ninja trying to take me out.* But this *wasn't* a baseball. It was larger. It was a softball. And it wasn't trying to take *me* out. It was trying to take the ninjas out. *Thwack.* I heard it again. My savior wasn't just yelling at these guys. My savior was chucking softballs at these guys.

My savior was a girl.

My savior was Maria Bonzer.

CHAPTER TWENTY

The ninjas of Griffith scampered off. I was still dazed, but I could hear their cleats clacking on the sidewalk. They were running away! It worked! Maria came over to me. She started helping me extract my arms from the bike rack. I must have looked like a puppy trapped in a storm drain.

I never thought I'd be so happy to see anyone in my life. Maria Bonzer was, yes, the niece of Mr. Bonzer the librarian. And yes, she is the Maria Bonzer me and the Mikes briefly thought was a murderer. But she ended up helping us solve the case last summer. I had no idea she was still in town.

"Whoa, Lenny, what happened to you?" she said.

"Are you . . . Are you real? Or . . . are . . . you . . . a . . . ?" Like I said, I was feeling woozy and was kind of afraid that I was imagining things. Like in movies when guys are lost in the desert and they start to get so hungry and thirsty that they think a cactus is a glass of water. A mirage! That's the word. I yelled it out. "Mirage!"

Maria laughed. "Yeah, Lenny. I'm a freaking mirage over here. You're tied to a bike rack hallucinating about the librarian's niece."

"Well, the first part *is* true," I said. "Though technically they didn't tie me up. I just sort of fell in."

"You did this to yourself?" she asked.

"No, not really. I mean, they were throwing baseballs at me! I was trying to get the heck out of here. One hit me in the back." I was trying not to cry and doing a not-okay job at it.

"It looks like one caught you in the face."

"That was that ninja's fist!" I said.

She laughed. "Um, do I have to call a doctor?" she said. "You really are seeing things."

"No," I said. "I'm fine. I know he wasn't actually a ninja. Just the way he had his hood up over his head. Looked kind of ninjalike."

"Got it," she said. "So those ninjas threw baseballs at you and then punched you in the face when you tried to flee on your bike?"

"Yeah," I said. "That pretty much sums it up."

"Why would they do that?" she asked. "Other than the fact that just about everyone who knows you wants to punch you in the face once in a while."

"Very funny," I said. "They did it because I'm onto their secret!"

"This sounds good," she said. "But I have to get home before dinner or my mom will kill me. Can you walk and talk?"

"Uh, sure," I said, just happy to stand. I was finally free of the bike rack. I spun the combination on the lock and popped the chain. It felt good to know that even if the ninjas returned, I could get out of there fast. However, they were nowhere to be found. Maria had successfully scared them off. I was a little embarrassed, but pretty grateful. My eye was killing me.

She pointed in the direction she was headed and I rode along. It's hard to ride that slowly, though, so I did that move where you stand over the bike but just walk rather than pushing the pedals. We walked like that while I gave her the scoop. The whole time my eye burned. I could feel it throbbing like a living thing was breathing on it. Breathing fire.

"So what are you doing here?" she said.

"I could ask you the same thing!" I said right back.

"Um, I go to school here?"

"You do?" I asked. It was a dumb question. She pointed to her own green Griffith sweatshirt. I had flashbacks of the ninja attack.

"Yeah. So what are you doing here?" she said again.

I filled her in. I told her all of it. About how Mike made the baseball team as a catcher after Famosa encouraged him. About how I helped him practice by throwing wild pitches and kicking him in the crotch. About how I got a job as the announcer for the Schwenkfelder games. And about how someone from Griffith was stealing Mike's signs, ripping off clues for the pitches from the great Hunter Ashwell.

"Whoa," she said. "You tell quite a tale."

I couldn't figure out if she was being sarcastic or not, so I just pressed on. "Yeah," I said. "Me and the Mikes have been working like crazy. Trying to figure the whole thing out."

"Have any luck?" she asked as we stopped at the busy intersection of Center Street.

"No," I said sadly.

"Hard to believe your brain trust wasn't having any success," she said. "I mean, especially given the fact that you don't have any brains."

"Ha," I said. "Har-har. Har-de-har-har. Har-de-freaking-har-freaking-har." That's the proper way to laugh sarcastically. No one ever says "har-de-har-har" in a nonsarcastic way. If they do, I don't want to know them.

"Well?" she said.

"Well, what?" I asked.

"I'm waiting."

"Waiting for what?" I asked. "Did you ask me a question?"

"I'm waiting for you to ask me a question," she said.

"If you're waiting for me to ask you to marry me," I said, "you're going to have to wait quite a bit longer. I should at least get my own car first." I don't know why I said that. It came out stupid. I started blushing.

"Har-de-freaking-har," she said. "You know what I'm waiting for you to ask."

"I honestly do not," I said.

"I'm waiting for you to ask me to help you."

"To help me?"

"Yeah," she said. She put her hand on her hip and spit. "We make a good team. You know that."

"It's true," I said. "We sort of did crack one of the biggest mysteries in Philadelphia sports history. I'm pretty sure we can get to the bottom of whatever shenanigans a bunch of middle school dorks can muster."

"That's like the pot calling the kettle a dork," she said.

"I'm not quite sure that's how the expression—"

"So you really think they're stealing your signs, huh?" she said. "They gotta be if they're hitting Ashwell. I hear that kid can throw."

"Yeah, yeah," I said. "I hear all about him all the time. Believe me. But before we get into this, you have to answer me something. Why are you going to help us?"

"What do you mean? I already told you. We make a good team."

"Yeah, but won't you be hurting your own team? You'll be helping Schwenkfelder beat Griffith."

"I have no loyalty to this stupid school," she said. "I never wanted to move to this stupid town anyway. No offense."

"Hey, don't apologize to me," I said. "If I was

Sam Schwenkfelder, sure, I'd be highly offended. But I'm not. I just live here. I didn't invent this stupid town."

"Was there really a Sam Schwenkfelder?" she asked.

"I don't know," I said. "But, listen, how do I know I can trust you with this?"

"It's the principle," she said.

"You think Principal Wagner is behind this? I could see *Vice* Principal Jaxheimer having a sideline as a criminal, but Wags seems pretty decent."

She rolled her eyes. "You know what I mean," she said. She spit into her hand and gestured for me to do the same.

I guess we were reaffirming our status as spit twins. Seemed good enough for me. "Put 'er there," I said. We shook on it. It was settled.

We were on the part of the road that doesn't have any sidewalk, so we were trying to stay close to the shoulder. I gave up riding and was pushing my bike as she was walking next to me. I looked around to make sure we weren't being watched.

"What are you so nervous about?" she asked.

"Just—those guys aren't going to cause trouble for you if they know you're working for the other side, are they?"

"They have no idea," she said. "Total double agent."

"Except that you did just kind of sort of call them 'idiots,'" I said.

She shrugged.

"Hey," I said. "Do you know who they are? Those guys, I mean."

"Well," she said. "I think our first clue is that they were members of the Griffith baseball team."

"Nice work, Sherlock," I said. "What tipped you off? The Griffith baseball sweatshirts they were wearing?"

She tapped the bill of her softball cap with her finger. "Always thinking," she said.

"Duh," I said. "I mean, did you recognize them?"

"No, I never saw their faces. They didn't stick around long, did they?" she asked. "Once they got a glimpse of my mighty arm."

"I didn't know you played softball," I said. "I thought you were just a fan."

"Why would you think that?" she asked.

"I don't know," I said. "You never mentioned it."

"You never asked," she said.

"No, I guess I didn't."

"There's a lot you don't know about me, Lenny Norbeck," she said.

"Yeah?" I said. "Well, there's a lot you don't know about me too."

"I know you spend all your time arguing with Mike and Other Mike. I know you love baseball and think you're some sort of detective, even though you get tangled up in a bike rack at the first sign of trouble. I know you're the announcer for the games over at Schwenkfelder. And I know you lose your library card all the time."

"That jerk Bonzer! What happened to the library code of secrecy?" I said.

She laughed. "That about sum it up?" she said.

"Yeah, pretty much." It was true. I was simple. "I guess the one with all the secrets is you. I didn't even know you were living here, for one. I thought you were just visiting for the summer and then it was back to the city."

"Yeah, that's what I thought too," she said. "That was the plan. Supposed to be anyway. But my mom decided she'd had enough of the city, I guess. Our apartment got broken into over the summer. My phone got taken. I miss it. Weird thing was, whoever stole it kept texting people I knew. Everyone was like, 'Why did you keep texting me?' I guess the thief just wanted to mess with me."

"Oh, jeez," I said. "Sorry to hear that. You catch the guy?"

"Nah," she said. "Gone without a trace."

"Should have hired a good detective," I said. "I think I can recommend one for next time."

"There never will be a next time," she said. "Now we're living out here with the cows and horses and dorks like you."

"Hey, excuse me," I said. "Things get pretty rough around here. Speaking of, how does my eye look?"

She stopped walking and I stopped the bike. She peered at my face for what felt like a long time. "You'll live," she said. "Working up a pretty decent bruise there, but you'll live. That's our house," she said, pointing up. "The one we're renting, I mean. There's lots of rich people around here. It's weird, we're, like, the only renters."

"Cool," I said, for some reason.

She shrugged. "Whatever."

"Whatever," I repeated.

"So keep me in the loop," she said. "Let me know how it's going. Keep me up to speed on any developments. Let me know if I can help. You know where to find me."

"I do?" I said.

"Um, yeah," she said, pointing up. "I just told you I live right there."

"Yeah," I said. "Got it. Cool." I am as smooth as a baby's butt.

She started up the steep set of concrete stairs toward the door. "One more thing," I called after her. "Would it help you to identify the ninjas if I told you something about how they talked?" I asked.

"Maybe," she said with a shrug.

"Their voices were . . . weird. Anybody on the team with an accent? Jagdish Sheth maybe?"

"Nah," she said. "Jagdish Sheth was born in New Jersey. Unless you count the New Jersey accent as weird."

"It wasn't Jersey-weird," I said. "It was . . . foreign somehow? German or Swedish or something?"

"How do I know what a Swedish accent sounds like?" she said.

"I don't know," I said. "Never mind."

"Do a Swedish accent," she said. "Do it right now."

"No," I said.

"That was a terrible Swedish accent."

"That was just me talking normal. I'm not saying they were necessarily Swedish, just that it sounded weird. It was like *well, well, well.*" I did my best to mimic the ninja's voice.

"That just sounds like someone doing a stupid voice," she said.

"Thanks for your help," I said.

She started to go in the house again.

"Wait—one *more* thing," I said.

"What's that?" she asked, rolling her eyes.

"Thanks for your help," I said. I hoped she knew I meant it.

She nodded once quickly and disappeared through the front door.

CHAPTER TWENTY-ONE

Maria lived just off of Center Street, so it was easy enough to find my way home. The journey was a little perilous, especially because it was getting dark and there were a lot of cars out. Well, a lot of cars for Schwenkfelder. I pedaled as fast as I could and was home in a matter of minutes.

I pulled my bike into the garage and walked into the house.

"Lenny, where were you?" my mom asked. She was standing in the kitchen washing dishes. I guess I missed dinner.

"I left you a note," I said. I pointed to the piece of paper stuck to the door.

"Yeah," she said. "And what language is this in?"

"Pretty much English," I said.

"Pretty much?" She held up the paper. My

handwriting has never been that great. And I was in sort of a rush to get to the library. She read it out loud. "It looks like it says 'At a wedding. Phil is dead.'"

I laughed. "Yeah, Mom. I went to a wedding after murdering some guy named Phil. Had to do it. Stupid Phil. You should have heard the stuff he was saying about you."

She did not laugh. She saw my eye. I tried to brush it off. I mean, I tried to brush *her* off. I did not try to brush my eye off. I like my eye. For seeing and stuff.

"It obviously says 'At the library. Phone is dead,'" I explained, trying to look away.

"That explains why you didn't pick up," she said. "I was nervous. And I think I had good reason! Lenny, what happened to your eye?" She grabbed me by the shoulders and peered at my face.

"Oh, this?" I said, pointing to the noninjured eye. "I was born like this. Had this guy since the very beginning. Good old right eye. Best friend of left eye. Thought you'd remember. There are plenty of pictures."

"Did someone hit you?" she asked. "Who hit you?"

"Nobody hit me, Mom," I said. It was such a lie.

"It was a baseball," I said. "Just horsing around. And sorry about the confusing note. But, hey, you should be proud. Maybe I *will* be a doctor like you and dad. I already have the bad handwriting."

"Yeah, but cardiologists are supposed to *cure* heart attacks, not cause them," she said. "You made me really worried." She handed me an ice pack.

Actually, it's not a pack but a frozen bear. We call him "Frosty Bear." I really need a new ice pack one of these days. It's hard to look tough with a frozen Frosty Bear on your eye.

"You say potato, I say potahto," I said.

"Speaking of," she said. "I have mashed potatoes if you're hungry."

"Mashed potahtoes," I said.

She laughed and scooped some on a plate. There was also some chicken, and I realized that, yes, I was hungry.

"Where's Dad?" I asked.

"Working late," she said. "He's not going to be happy when he sees this eye."

"We'll just tell him that the other guy is much worse off," I said. "Because when I find out who did this? He will be."

"I thought you told me it was a baseball?" she said, peering at me.

Uh-oh. That's why I'm bad at lying. You always have to remember the lie you told, and sometimes stuff just comes out of my mouth. I tried to pretend it was a joke.

"Ha-ha," I said. "Just kidding." Smooth.

She gave me her skeptical mom eye, which I tried to ignore while I wolfed down my food. After I ate, I had to go up to my room to work on the case. It was no longer about just stealing signs.

It was getting personal.

CHAPTER TWENTY-TWO

I went up to my room with Frosty Bear on my eye and grabbed the phone. I put my feet up on my desk. Not sure why, but this is what detectives always do. Something about putting your feet up means being a detective. It probably helps you think. It was kind of uncomfortable. I put my feet back down. Detectives are also always smoking, but we know that's not an option. The cardiologists would murder me; plus, cigarettes are gross. I thought it would be cool to casually throw a ball up and down, but I kind of suck at catching. There was the distinct possibility I'd take an actual baseball to the other eye and end up looking like a raccoon.

So I just sat there cross-legged like a dork on my Phillies comforter and dialed the phone.

"Hello," Mike said.

"Yeah, who dis?" I asked in a tough voice. I was

feeling pretty rattled from the punching incident, but also sort of silly.

"You called me, Lenny," he said.

"How you know it's me?" I asked, still using the rough voice.

"Caller ID," he said. "Also, why are you talking like that?"

"I'm your rough-talking detective," I said. "I'm dangerous, but fair. I want just two things: justice and a cough drop."

"You sound more like a criminal," he said.

"Well, I ain't."

I could almost hear his eyes rolling through the phone. "So what do you got for me, Detective?" he asked. "Anything?"

"I got all I ever needed," I said. "A library card, a black eye, and a hunch."

"What?" he said. "Stop talking in that weird voice and explain to me what's going on. And what do you mean a black eye?"

"Ninjas," I said with a sigh. "It was ninjas."

"Dude, shut up," he said.

"It really was!" I said. "Okay, not *really*, but I thought it was. And some kid from Griffith really did punch me in the eye."

"What?"

I told him the whole harrowing tale. I didn't exactly say Maria *saved* me, but I did have to mention that she was there. I figured it would probably come up later.

"Wow," he said. "Ninjas."

"And I did go to the library today and get a book about how to cheat at baseball. Pretty fascinating stuff."

"I bet," he said.

"And the weird thing is, someone had it out just before me."

"Who?" he asked excitedly.

"Bonzer wouldn't tell me," I said.

"Stupid librarian code of honor."

"Exactly," I said.

He sighed again. There was a lull in the conversation. I had to get down to business. I had to get down to brass tacks. Why do people get down to brass tacks? I've never even seen a brass tack. Anyway, I didn't want to ask him the hard questions. No one ever said being a detective would be easy. But I had a strong feeling Davis was framed. And an even stronger feeling who framed him. But just trying to say it was impossible. I felt a baseball-sized lump in my throat.

I took a deep breath and let it rip: "Before we

get too much further into this, I need to ask you a few questions," I said.

"What? Who? Me?" he said.

"Yes," I said.

"Sure, sure," he said. He sounded distracted. Like maybe he wanted to change the topic but couldn't figure out how to do so. I pressed on. No hard questions to start. Just easy ones. I thought it would be cool to get out a notepad to scribble ideas like detectives do, but I couldn't find one. I just promised myself I'd remember everything he said.

"Quick question that came to me," I said. "Why do you and Hunter need signs anyway?"

"The two pitches," Mike said. "He throws the fastball and the palmball."

"Yeah," I said. "I know that. But if you're so good at catching everything, why don't you just get rid of the signs and block everything he throws? Then the batter would never know what's coming."

"It's not that easy, Len," Mike said. I could hear his voice rising. He was getting aggravated. "The two pitches are very different. The palmball is superslow and breaks a little. The fastball comes whistling in. If I don't have the glove in the right place, every pitch would smack me in the chest."

"Or in the newts," I said.

"Exactly. Plus, Hunter is just weird about it. He can't decide what pitch to throw and when. He totally needs me to call the game for him."

"Okay, okay," I said. "This leads me to my next question. Why don't you guys make up a new system?"

"You don't think I've thought of that?" Mike said. "I've discussed changing our code, like, twenty times with Hunter. He refuses! Also, if you had any idea how long it took him to learn one system, you'd never ask that we make up a new one. Or come up with rolling signs that change. Forget it."

"So what you're saying," I said, drawing out the word, "is that Hunter Ashwell is *not* a genius."

"I meant he's a genius on the mound, Lenny," he said. "Not in the classroom. He thinks algebra is a woman's article of clothing that fell in a fish tank."

"Algae-bra?" I said. "Good one."

"Yeah," he said without laughing. "I heard that from my dad."

So I was cooking up two theories. Sort of the same theory. It started with this: Davis Gannett was innocent of stealing the phone. It was planted in his bag like he said.

It was planted there by Mike.

And so then Davis Gannett got kicked off the team, just like Mike wanted. This made Davis angry. Who wouldn't get a little angry about that? You're framed for a crime and kicked off the team. The guy who got you booted takes your place and gets all the glory. So how does this tie in to the other theory? One word: *revenge*.

If anyone would know how to steal signals from Schwenkfelder, who better than Schwenkfelder's own former catcher? *The Semilegal Guide to Cheating at Baseball* had taught me that. You had to be particularly wary when a catcher went over to the other side. They knew all your signs, all your secrets. This was just like that! Davis went over to Griffith and helped them set up a system to steal Mike's signs. When the batters knew what was coming, Hunter was easy to hit off of. Davis could sit there and laugh, living it up. He actually came over to our bench after the game to gloat about it. Maybe he even knew Mike was the one who set him up.

So, how to prove it? Step one was to interrogate Suspect A. Seriously weird. The suspect was my best friend. I couldn't believe it. But I had to get some more information from Mike.

"So listen," I said into the phone. "I've been

thinking that somehow Davis could be involved in this." Not exactly hard-hitting to begin with, but I was working up to it.

"Yeah?" Mike said. "Yeah! It makes perfect sense."

"It does," I said. "Indeed, it does. He is definitely the prime suspect in the sign-stealing scheme. But here's something else I'm thinking about: What if he got kicked off the team based on some, shall we say, *false information?*"

"What?"

"What if he was innocent?" I said. There. Blunt.

"They found the phone in *his* shin guard!" Mike said, his voice rising. "No one else would ever touch that thing. It smells terrible."

"Davis has smelly shins?"

"Davis has smelly everything," Mike said. "Trust me. Everything about that dude stinks."

"I know, I know," I said. Then I paused and took a deep breath. "But what I'm saying is: What if he was *framed?* What if—I don't know—maybe, like, Kyle's dad made the whole thing up? Or what if somebody else framed him, you know? *Framed him?*"

Mike said nothing. I didn't want to keep saying

"framed." It wasn't very subtle. The phone was silent for so long I thought the battery had gone dead. "Are you still there? Maybe the person had a perfectly good reason—I don't know." Still nothing. "Hello?" I said.

He sighed. "Yeah, I'm here," he said. "But I really should go. I got homework." He said it so fast it sounded like one word. And with that, he hung up.

I sat there peering at the phone with a skeptical eye. *Mike doing homework?* That was fishier than a cat burp. I peered again. Peering felt weird. My eye was still hurting, but that wasn't the worst of my problems. My stomach was hurting too. My chest was hurting. My *brain* was hurting. I was hurting all over. I took a deep breath and tried to sort things out. I ran the information backward and forward a million times. Unfortunately, I kept coming up with the same results.

It all made perfect sense. Who had something to gain from Davis getting kicked off the team? Who had been praying for his big chance to be a starting catcher? Who had the means, the motive, and the opportunity? All the same guy. My best friend.

It felt so weird to think it. The best suspect here was without a doubt Mike. But Mike wasn't the type. And Davis *was* the criminal type. He smelled bad for sure. Shins and all. Who knows? Maybe Davis was even there when I was attacked. Maybe he was one of the ninjas! He was there to work on his spy gig, posing as a guy from Griffith. It all made perfect sense!

Except for one thing.

Davis had been hanging out with Other Mike the whole time.

Unless that too was a lie.

My head was spinning. Was it possible that not just one but two Mikes were lying to me? Both caught up in a complicated web of lies? Both were lying liars who just wanted to keep lying out of their lying faces? Who was I supposed to turn to? Who could I trust?

Just then, my dad stuck his head in the door.

"Something troubling you, son?" he said.

"Oh, hey, Dad," I said. "Kind of."

"Is it your eye? Sheesh. That looks pretty bad. Mom said it was a baseball. Are you telling us the truth? It looks sort of the size and shape of a fist."

"Yeah, well, a baseball *is* the size and shape of a fist, if you haven't noticed."

"Oh, I've noticed," he said. "But I've also had a few shiners in my day. I know what they look like."

"*Shiners?*" I said.

"Yeah, you know—a black eye. From getting punched. I'm not sure why they call them shiners. They just do."

"You've had a few shiners in your day?" I asked. I was genuinely curious. It was hard to imagine my mild-mannered doctor father getting in a fistfight. I wasn't trying to change the subject away from *my* shiner. Okay, maybe I was a little. But I wanted to hear the story too.

"Yeah, you know," he said. "Just stupid fights. One time a kid kept calling me String Bean. I used to be really skinny, you know?"

"I find that hard to believe," I said. Dad wasn't fat, but he had a pretty sizable belly, which hung around his waist like an overstuffed pillow.

"Yeah," Dad said. "I do like cake." He patted his belly.

"Calling you String Bean made you so mad that you hit a guy?"

"Well, kind of," he said. "I pushed him. Before I knew what happened, he punched me in the eye. Gave me a nasty shiner."

"How old were you?" I asked.

"Oh, about your age," he said. "I was too embarrassed to tell Grandpa. So I made up a lie about tripping and falling onto an orange."

I laughed. "You are a terrible liar," I said.

"Yeah," he said with a laugh. "That's one trait I wish you'd inherited instead of just my dashing good looks. You're too good at lying. It's troublesome."

"Not lying," I said, lying. I pointed to my eye. "Just a baseball. I've been helping Mike practice. Throwing him some cheese."

"You know I threw some serious cheese back in my day?" he said.

"So you claim," I said.

"My best pitch, though, was the Vulcan change."

I looked at him skeptically. He held his hand up like the guy from *Star Trek*. Two fingers together on each side with a space in the middle like scissors fingers.

"You're making that up," I said.

"Total real pitch," he said. He grabbed a ball off my dresser and sort of lodged it in there and went into a windup. "Live long and prosper!" he yelled, pretending to throw the pitch.

"You are an idiot," I said with a smile.

"It's the batter who looks like an idiot," he said. "Works every time." He raised his arm like an umpire. "Strike three with the Vulcan change! The crowd goes wild!" Then he got all serious out of nowhere in that weird dad way. "You know, you can talk to me about anything," he said.

"Yeah," I said. "I know." I paused. I wanted to tell him. But I couldn't *tell* him. I tried to keep it vague. "So listen," I said. "If, let's say, there was maybe someone that you trusted—like really trusted—but you maybe suspect that maybe they did something, like, kind of bad—like maybe pretty bad—what would you do?"

Dad paused. He sighed. He rubbed his hand across his dome. "I think you know the answer, Len," he said.

"You tell someone?" I said.

"No," he said. "You talk to them about it."

This was not the answer I expected.

"Listen," he said. "If it's something serious, like this person is hurting themselves or doing something major, then, yeah, you tell a grown-up. You tell me right now. But if it's something that a friend is doing—I'm sorry, *maybe* doing—and you need to find out, you talk to them about it. Man to man."

It sounded so heavy in my heart. I knew it had to be true. It was also the first time Dad had ever referred to me as a man. Felt pretty good.

"Oh," Dad said. "I almost forgot. There was a message on the machine for you from before. Some kid from school."

"Who?" I asked.

"Kyle Webb," he said.

"Weird," I said.

"No," he said. *"Webb."*

"You're hilarious, Dad," I said in a tone that I hoped made it pretty clear I was kidding.

Dad seemed to not get it, though. He grinned like he was really proud of himself. "I know," he said. "So who is this Kyle Weird?" He handed me the piece of paper he had taken the message on. It had Kyle's name and phone number.

"Skinny guy. Plays first base. No idea why he called me."

"Gonna call him back?"

"Maybe," I said.

"Just don't call him String Bean," Dad said.

"Got it," I said.

Dad finally left the room. I had no idea what Kyle wanted or even how he got my number. He was relatively new to school—not someone I grew up with or spent a lot of time hanging out with or anything. Why was he calling me? What did he want? I would have to wait to find out. It was time to call Mike. Man to man.

CHAPTER TWENTY-THREE

I dialed the number I knew so well. It rang a few times. Mike's sister, Arianna, picked up the phone. "Hello?" she said.

"Is Mike there?" I asked.

"Who may I say is calling?" she said.

"Ari, it's Lenny."

"Lenny who?" she asked.

"Lenny Norbeck," I said.

"Lenny Norbeck who?" she said.

"Lenny Norbeck, the person who is going to make your life miserable if you don't give your brother the phone, that's who!" She was seriously the most annoying person in the world.

"Sheesh," she said. "Who pooped in your milk?"

After a few seconds Mike was back on the line. "Hello?" he said.

"Hey, it's Len," I said.

"I know," he said. "No one else gets Arianna as angry as you."

"Why does she hate me so much?" I said.

"Probably your face," Mike offered helpfully. "So, listen, didn't you just call, like, five minutes ago? What is going on here?"

"Mike," I said. "About the whole thing with Kyle's dad's phone . . . is there something you want to tell me?" I asked.

"No," he said. "Not really."

"Nothing?" I asked.

"Listen, Lenny," he said, "if you're accusing me of something, just go ahead and accuse me."

There was a pause and then I blurted it out.

"I think you took Mr. Webb's phone and put it in Davis's shin guard to get Davis kicked off the team." There was no response, so I kept talking. "I totally get it," I said. "Davis is a jerk; plus, you wanted to be the starting catcher. No one can blame you, really. Two birds, one stone."

There was silence on the other end. Then Mike spoke slowly, in a voice shaky with anger. "The only bird here, Lenny," he said, "is the one I'm giving you."

"What?" I said.

"I'm giving you the bird into the phone. You can't see it. Trust me. I am."

"Why are you doing that?" I said.

"Why do you think?" he said. "You're supposed to be my best friend! We've been friends our whole lives! And you think I'm a thief?"

"I'm not saying you're a thief," I said. "Just that you had one second where you, uh—"

"Stole something? Because that kind of is the definition of a thief."

"I think you knew they'd find it. I think you knew Mr. Webb would get it back. It wasn't about stealing. You didn't even keep the phone."

"Because I didn't *take* the phone!" he screamed. "I'm not a thief and I'm not the kind of person who would frame a teammate to get a starting job. And you know what else I'm not?" he said.

"A ballerina?" I ventured, going for a joke.

"Your friend," he said. "I'm not your friend. Not anymore. Good-bye, Lenny. Don't call back."

CHAPTER TWENTY-FOUR

My head was reeling. What did Mike mean that he wasn't my friend anymore? Sure, it wasn't the first time he had said something like that. It wasn't the first time he had said *exactly* that. When you're friends with someone for as long as we've been friends, you fight sometimes. And then five minutes later you make up. But this felt different. This didn't feel like when we were six and we'd get into a huge argument about who got to be Spider-Man. This was serious stuff. I had accused Mike of something pretty bad. And he was pretty mad. And I was pretty sad. Even rhyming wasn't going to cheer me up.

I was just zoning out in my room, lying on the bed. I still had the piece of paper with Kyle's number on it. I doubted he would cheer me up. Talking to Kyle was just about the most depressing thing you could do. But what's the expression? Misery loves company? I sure was miserable. Might as well have some company.

I dialed the number. "Hello?" said a glum voice on the other end. It sounded like a talking rain cloud, so I knew it was Kyle.

"Hey, Kyle," I said. "It's Lenny Norbeck. You called?"

"Oh, hey, Lenny, yeah," he said.

"Um, did you have a, uh, reason for calling or . . . ?"

"I don't know," he said. "The rumor around school is that you're some sort of detective."

"Yeah?" I said. "Well, not anymore. The detective game doesn't lead to anything but trouble." I thought about telling him how Mike was mad at me, but I didn't want to drag Kyle into this. More to the point, I didn't want to drag Kyle's dad back into this. If he found out it was really Mike and not Davis who took the phone, well, let's just say there would be trouble. More trouble. Maybe Mike didn't want to be my friend anymore, but I still didn't want to have Mr. Webb on his case.

"Too bad," Kyle said.

My curiosity kicked in. "Why?" I said. "You have a case for me?"

"Maybe," he said. "Sort of . . ."

"I'm listening."

"I thought you were done being a detective."

"Maybe I am, maybe I'm not," I said. I didn't want trouble, but I did want a distraction. Kyle's case might be something interesting. Something different to think about.

"Well, I'm not really sure if this is a case for a detective, but I just . . . I don't know who else to call."

"Spill it," I said, going back to my detective voice.

"Well, I want to get my parents back together. The divorce, Lenny, it's killing me. I know they can get back together. I just know it."

I didn't want to say anything. I had seen enough movies to know that this kind of thing never works. Kids can't save their parents' marriages and no one ever has a cell phone signal when a bad guy is around. These are the two things I've learned from movies. But I didn't want to say anything. Kyle seemed so desperate. I just made a noncommittal *um-hurm* sort of noise.

Kyle continued. "I think somehow if I get a message to my mom and make her think it's from my dad apologizing, that would just be enough.

That would get it all started and it would go from there."

"Um-hurm," I said again.

"So do you think you can help me?" he said. "I, uh, I can pay you."

"You had me at 'pay you,'" I said.

"That was the last thing I said. You can't say 'You had me' about the last thing. It's supposed to be the first thing."

"Well, okay then!" I said.

"So you'll take the case?" he said.

"I'll tell you what," I said. "I'll think about it. If I come up with something, you'll hear from me."

He told me his address and again I wished I had a notebook. I didn't have any desire to take this impossible, ridiculous case Kyle was trying to hand me. But I did want to write something else down. He was giving me . . . a clue.

CHAPTER TWENTY-FIVE

It was Saturday. I had a few cases cooking. But nothing going on with any of them. Not really. I wasn't sure where to go next. Why wasn't real life more like baseball? You just try to go from base to base until you're home. Just score more runs than the other team and you win. Solving cases wasn't like that. Life wasn't like that. You never knew which direction things would fly off in. And sometimes even if you got what you were looking for, you'd find you didn't want it at all. . . . Okay, there was also Kyle's case. . . . Well, was that even a case? Maybe a job for a spy, not a detective. I told him I'd think about it, but that was a lie.

I wasn't coming up with anything in my sign-stealing investigation either. I had some theories—at least I thought I did. But I couldn't prove any of it. Plus, I really didn't want to get punched in the face again. It was so weird. I couldn't turn to Mike for help. I couldn't turn to Other Mike either. I honestly had no idea what to do.

I sort of wanted to talk to my dad about it, but somehow the conversation would come back to my "shiner." I was already committed to that lie. I enjoyed a certain amount of freedom and didn't want to compromise it. Would they let me go off on my own if they knew I was sneaking around, investigating crimes, getting shiners? No, they would not.

So I had nowhere else to turn but to Maria Bonzer.

I didn't have her phone number or email or anything, but I did know where she lived. And I had nothing to lose. It was a slow Saturday at the Norbeck house. I don't know if I mentioned this before or not, but my mom GOT RID OF, LIKE, ALL MY TOYS. So I decided to bust out the bike and go knock on Maria's door.

I couldn't help but feel nervous on the ride over there. It was close to Griffith Middle School, which meant it was close to where I got punched in the face. I didn't like to admit it, but it was sort of traumatic. I kept my eyes peeled for ninjas, or anyone else who might want to fight me.

I crossed Center Street and found Maria's house, at least the one I thought was hers. They kind of all looked the same. Thankfully, there was a Phillies flag stuck in the planters outside the one I was pretty sure was hers. I rang the doorbell and waited.

Two seconds later, she opened the door.

Three seconds later, she slammed the door.

Then she opened it again. "Ha-ha, just kidding, Lenny. What's up?"

"Nothing," I said. "What's up with you?"

"Nothing? You're the one who rode your bike all the way over here. You must want to talk to me about something. You have any developments in the case?"

"Developments in the— No. Can I come in?"

She looked back over her shoulder and seemed to think about it for a while. "How about I come out there?" she said. "Just let me find some shoes."

I stood outside the door for what seemed like way too long. Maybe she didn't really want to talk to me. Maybe shoes were really hard to find. Girls were strange, that much was obvious.

Finally she showed back up at the door. "Let's walk and talk," she said.

"Took you long enough," I said.

"Things are weird at home," she said.

I didn't ask for additional information, but she offered it anyway. "My parents used to fight all the time. Then they got a divorce. For the longest time I would have done anything to get them back together. I used to have crazy plans, like if I could just trick them or something. . . . Anyway, my mom's doing much better. But she really hates men, I think. Boys too."

"Sorry?" I said.

"That's okay," she said. "I assured her that you weren't really a boy."

"Thanks?" I said.

"You know what I mean," she said, and punched me in the arm. I suspected that I *did* know what she meant, but I wasn't sure I liked it. I didn't have time to dwell on it, because she started peppering me with questions.

"When is Hunter's next game?" she asked.

"Wednesday," I said. "Against Highland."

"Okay, fine. If he pitches well there, we know what that means."

"What?"

"That Griffith *was* stealing signs."

"Yeah, probably," I said. "Or that Highland stinks like rotten eggs."

"Do you have any leads? Any suspects?" she asked.

"Well, just the one," I said. I told her about how Davis got kicked off the team for stealing. And about how he comes to all the games.

Then I told her all about how—and why—I suspected Mike of framing Davis. I told her how we had a big fight and how he said we weren't friends anymore.

"So why did you just tell me that whole thing about how Davis did it?"

"I don't know," I said. "I'm just trying to convince myself."

"But you are convinced it was Mike?" she asked.

"Pretty convinced," I said.

"That's seriously messed up," she said.

"I know," I said. "That's why I'm asking you for help."

"This was a wise choice," she said with an evil grin.

"Hey," I said. "Didn't you say that your phone got stolen back in Philly?"

"Yeah," she said.

"Think they're connected?" I asked.

"Um, they're all connected, because everyone in the world has a phone these days. That's like saying that because that one guy has a face and that other guy has a face, they must be brothers."

"Totally," I said.

"Are you even listening?" she asked.

"Yeah, I'm listening. Totally. Total face brothers." But the truth is, I *wasn't* listening. I was thinking. Dangerous, I know. I was doing some *good* thinking. Then I was yelling. "I think I solved the case!"

"You know who was stealing Schwenkfelder's signs and how?" Maria said, coming to an abrupt stop on the sidewalk. She turned to face me.

"No!" I said.

"You know who but not how?"

"No!"

"You know how but not who?"

"No!" I said again. I knew it was getting annoying, but I couldn't stop. "I know neither who nor how," I said. "I have solved the other case."

"Is it the question of who the most annoying person in the universe is?" she asked, starting to walk again. "Because I think I have solved that one too."

"The case I have solved is the question of the missing cell phone. Now, I don't like Davis Gannett and you don't either," I said.

"I have never met him," she said. Not helpful.

"Whatever," I said. "The point is this: He's a jerk. And I wanted to believe that he was the one who stole the phone. We all wanted that. But he insisted that he was innocent, and Other Mike believed him."

"Personally, I'm not totally sure we should trust Other Mike's perspective on this or anything else," she said. "But carry on."

"Other Mike is kind of a genius, if you haven't noticed," I said.

"I haven't," she said.

"Well, he said he thought Davis was innocent, and that someone else must have been the one to steal the phone. That's why I started to suspect Mike. But it wasn't Mike."

"Yes, but *who?*" she said, her voice dripping with sarcasm. I ignored the sarcasm.

"Yes," I said. "That is the question. Who else would steal Kyle Webb's father's cell phone? And why?"

"Yes," she said. "Those are the questions."

"Well, don't ask me," I said. "Let's go ask the thief."

CHAPTER TWENTY-SIX

I really did wish I had that notebook. As it was, I had to trust my memory. There are trustier things out there, let me tell you that much. But I thought I remembered the address, more or less. Something with some fours and fives in it anyway. "Come on, Maria," I said. "Let's go to Kyle Webb's house."

"What?" she said. "Didn't you just say Kyle was the guy who had his phone stolen? And we're going to see the thief? Who steals their own phone?"

"Not *his* own phone," I said. "His dad's."

"What's he going to do with his own dad's cell phone? Like his dad wouldn't find out?"

"Not to keep it permanently," I said. "He just wanted to use it for a little while. Like how you said the jerk who stole your phone kept texting people you knew? What if that's what Kyle wanted to do?"

"Why would Kyle want to text people who know *me*?"

"No, Kyle wanted to text people from his *dad's* address book. Kyle wanted to text people *pretending* to be his dad! Specifically, Kyle's mom. Remember how you said you wanted to trick your parents into getting back together? That's what Kyle was doing. His parents were going through a divorce. Kyle thought he could save the marriage, keep them together. He told me as much. He asked me to help him. I'll bet he thought he could swipe his dad's phone and start secretly sending friendly texts. Like 'Oh, I'm so sorry, I still want to be married to you, kissy kissy hug hug.'"

"*Kissy kissy hug hug?*" Maria said, arching an eyebrow. "Is that how you text, Lenny?"

I blushed. "What? Me? No. Of course not. But the point is, that's exactly how Kyle would text *if* he was pretending to be his dad. Trying to get back together with his mom!"

"So then, what—his dad came into the locker room? And Kyle was afraid he'd be seen with it? So he stashed it the first place he could think of?"

"Right. He stashed it in Davis's shin guard. Kyle's dad is truly terrifying, so Kyle definitely didn't want it to come out that he was the one who took the phone. His dad would kill him! Mr. Webb basically wanted to murder Kyle when he dropped a pop-up. In foul territory! Plus, Kyle didn't love Davis. Nobody did. Two birds, one stone."

I felt a huge weight off my back. I could literally breathe easier. Phew. It was so nice to know that Mike wasn't the one who framed Davis! It was like having my old friend back. Not that he *was* my friend. I was going to have to apologize. The thought did not sit well. I tried to stop having it.

Thankfully, I got distracted. "There," I said, really proud of myself. "Kyle Webb's house."

"How do you know?" Maria said.

"A good detective knows everything," I said. "Plus, that's Kyle in the driveway." I pointed. He was throwing a baseball to himself and catching it. Just launching it up underhand and waiting for it to fall. Alone. That's always kind of a sad thing to see. It was, like, even more sad because you knew his dad was a jerk.

"Wow," Maria said to me. "You truly are the Sherlock Holmes of suburbia." Then she yelled, "I got it!" toward Kyle.

It startled him and he dropped the ball. It was kind of mean, but I laughed. Kyle looked sheepish.

"Oh, hey, Lenny," he said, squinting to recognize me.

"Hi, Kyle," I said once we were closer. "This is Maria Bonzer. Her uncle is the librarian."

"That's right," she said. "Try to contain your excitement."

Kyle gave me a puzzled look. "So what's up? Did you, uh, think about what we talked about?"

"You don't have to be secretive," I said. "Maria is a detective too. She works for me."

She gave me a look that would have killed a lesser man.

"*With* me?" I tried. "I work *for* her, I mean?"

She laughed. "Listen, we just work together," she said. "And we know all about the little game you're playing here—and I don't mean catch."

"Excuse me?" Kyle said.

"Oh, okay, Maria," I said. "Let's just slow down and—" But I should have known. With Maria Bonzer there was no such thing as slowing down.

"We know all about how you took your dad's phone," she said.

Kyle gave her a dumb look. That might have been his normal look. I don't know. It seemed, like, extra-dumb. What if we were wrong? You can't just go around accusing people of things.

"Why would I—?" Kyle started to say.

"Oh, don't play dumb," she said. "Even though I can see that you are quite good at it. You want your parents back together. I get that. Ain't no crime. So you swipe Daddy's phone. Send a text to Mom. 'Oh, I'm sorry. Kissy kissy hug hug.'"

"*Kissy kissy hug hug?*" Kyle said slowly.

"Those are Lenny's words," Maria said.

"Hey, I—" I started.

"Lenny?" Kyle asked. His voice sounded so sad. "I hire you and this is how you treat me? You think I was the one who"—he lowered his voice to a whisper—"stole my own dad's phone?"

"Why are you whispering?" Maria said.

"He doesn't want his dad to hear," I said. "He's kind of mean." Then to Kyle I added, "No offense."

"None taken," he said, still whispering. "Believe me. I know. He has a temper these days."

"Yeah, but why are you whispering unless you don't want your dad to find out the truth?" Maria was talking louder and louder, aiming her words toward an open window.

"Keep it down!" Kyle said.

"Well," Maria said. "Either you have something to hide or you don't."

And with that, Kyle started to cry.

CHAPTER TWENTY-SEVEN

"Gee, that went well," I said to Maria as we walked back toward her house.

"Yeah," she said. "If you like seeing dudes cry."

"I mean, Mike is innocent! I can't wait to tell him."

Shortly after he spilled his tears, Kyle spilled everything. He was trying to take his dad's phone just so he could text his mom. He got caught in the act and stashed the phone the first place he found. Just so happened to be Davis's smelly shin guard.

He only cried a little. Well, first he denied it, then he cried. Then he told us not to tell anyone, then he cried again. Then he said his dad was going to murder him if he found out. Maria said, "Probably." Then he said Davis was going to murder him if he found out. Maria said, "Probably," again. And then he cried again. Okay, he in fact cried a lot. She tried to console him by pointing out that you actually can't get murdered twice. Shockingly, this did not make him feel better.

But then I came up with a pretty sweet solution.

"All you have to do is tell Coach Zo what really happened," I said. "Resign from the team like a man and he won't mention it to your dad if you ask him not to. And we won't say anything."

"What about Davis?" Kyle asked, his voice snotty with tears.

"Don't worry about him," I said. "I'll handle Davis Gannett." Though of course I had no idea how. . . .

We walked in silence for a minute. "Wait," Maria said. "If the truth gets out there, won't Davis be back on the team? Won't Mike lose his starting job?"

What was I thinking? I got so caught up in solving the case that I missed this obvious outcome. It was wrong that Davis got kicked off the team for something he didn't do. But of course the other side of that coin was also obvious. If Davis got back on the team, Mike would probably lose his starting spot. Mike was already mad at me! He already said we weren't friends. Being the starting catcher on this team meant so much to him! His whole future rode on it. Well, at least high school. He would kill me if I ruined it for him. And what did I owe Davis Gannett anyway? All he ever did was call me a dork-bucket and try to make my life miserable.

"Maybe we should go back and tell Kyle not to say anything to Coach Zo," I said.

"We're detectives," she said. "We just find out the truth. If people don't like it, that doesn't make it not true."

I offered to accompany Maria home. I didn't actually say it that dorkily. Like I'd really be like, "Oh, madam, can I accompany you home?" Fine, actually I did say something like that. Okay, exactly that.

She gave me a horrible and disgusted look. "Dude, you live that way—I live this way. You think I can't make it home by myself?"

"No, I just . . . W-well . . ." I was stammering. "I was just asking to be nice! You don't have to be so shocked. You made a face like I offered to fart on your cat."

She repeated the look. "You truly are weird, Lenny," she said. "You know that?"

"Whatever. Thanks for your help. We still don't know how that evil new school of yours is stealing signs, but we're onto something."

"Also, you're *on* something," she said.

I buckled my helmet and rode off.

I decided to ride straight to Mike's house. This couldn't be discussed by text. This couldn't be discussed over the phone. This was a man-to-man situation if there ever was one. As I pedaled there, I thought back to the winter for some reason. I thought back to the day I made this same trip in order to kick him in the crotch. It seemed like so long ago, yet was really just a few months. Since then he had risen from a guy getting crotch-kicked in the garage to the starting lineup, catching a perfect game. And now I had to go simultaneously apologize and deliver the news that it would all be over? First I accuse him of a crime he didn't commit and then I help him lose his starting role? Would I want to be my friend if I were him?

I dropped my bike in the driveway and rang the doorbell. As always, Mike's mom answered. As always, she told me I didn't need to ring the doorbell. As always, Mike's little sister was standing there, sticking her tongue out at me.

"Is Mike home?" I asked.

"Up in his room," Arianna said. "Why so glum, Lenny? Your dog die?"

"I don't have a dog," I said flatly.

"I know," she said. "It's called a joke."

I didn't laugh. I just trudged upstairs to Mike's room. I stuck my head in the door carefully, like it might get bitten off. Mike was sitting on the floor, playing a handheld video game. He looked up, saw me, then looked back to the screen. His face showed nothing. He said nothing. He was acting like we weren't friends. Heck, he was acting like we never even met each other.

"Uh, hey, Mike, listen," I said. "Do you have a second?"

He said nothing. All I could hear was the faint video-game music.

I swallowed hard and continued. "Hey, well, so, listen," I said. "I really just have to say—"

"The only thing I want to hear you say," he said through gritted teeth, "is good-bye."

"Mike," I pleaded. "Come on. Let me explain."

"If you don't want two black eyes," he said, "you'll be leaving now."

Mike was strong and had spent a lot of time

toughening up his hands. If he wanted to give me a black eye—or worse—there was nothing I could do to stop him.

I sighed. "You know what," I said. "I deserve that."

"You're right you do!" he said. He threw the video game onto his bed and jumped up. He was a little bit shorter than me, but he drew himself up to his full height and got right in my face.

"Fine," I said. "I'm going to say I'm sorry and then you can hit me if you want." I closed my eyes and said, "I'm sorry." I waited for his fist. "I've been hit once. I can handle it again." Don't get me wrong: I didn't *want* to handle it again. But I figured I probably could. I figured I deserved it.

Nothing happened.

I must have taken him slightly off guard. I opened my good eye halfway and peeked at him. "I'm really sorry, Mike," I said. "I suspected you of something you didn't do. I was a bad friend. I'll never doubt you again. I promise."

"Um, thanks," he said. He took a step back. He unclenched his fist.

"Don't thank me yet," I said.

"Why?" His right fist reclenched, if that's a word.

"Well, the reason I'm apologizing . . . I mean,

part of the reason . . . is that I figured out who *did* steal Kyle's dad's phone."

"Oh yeah?" he asked.

"Yeah," I said.

"And it wasn't Davis Gannett?"

"No. Kyle stole his own dad's phone."

"Why on earth would he do that?"

I explained the whole thing to Mike. He said nothing. He went back to playing his game.

Then he spoke. He didn't look up. It was like he was talking to the guys on the screen and not to me. "All along I sort of thought that it wasn't really Davis. I mean, I didn't know *who* it was! And I wasn't sure. I didn't have proof or anything. I just . . . Well, Davis was behind the plate with me most of that practice. There was hardly any chance for him to get near the bleachers, to steal a phone. Plus, why would he hide it where it was sure to be found?"

"Yeah," I said. "So why didn't you say anything?"

"Isn't it obvious?" he said glumly.

"You were happy that Davis got thrown off the team? So you could be the starting catcher?"

"Does that make me a bad person?" Mike said, nodding, biting his lip.

"Nah," I said. "I don't think so. I think anyone would have done the same."

"Not you, Lenny. You're so good."

"So why do I feel so bad?" I said.

"Because you helped your best friend lose his starting job to a maniac milk-pooper?" he said.

"Oh yeah," I said. "That."

"Hey," he said, "I'm all for anything that makes us a better team. And besides, there's always next year."

"Yeah," I said. "Next year."

CHAPTER TWENTY-EIGHT

Monday. Lunch. Me and Mike and Other Mike. Once again we were talking about the mystery of the stolen signs. Life was like that. As soon as you solved one mystery, there was another one waiting for you. Mike and I were racking our brains, trying to figure out what to do. There was no game that day. Highland and Griffith were playing over at Highland, giving the Mustangs the day off.

"Hey, so can I help with this whole thing or what?" Other Mike said, looking up from his book.

"Um, sure," Mike said.

"I doubt the culprit is a warlock," I said. "We don't need someone to cast a counterspell."

"Ha-ha," Other Mike said. "Though I could tell you that the warlocks in *Warlock Wallop* do have a sophisticated ball game of sorts that they play called 'Spurious,' which you might actually enjoy if you bothered to give it a try. They hit the ball with a bat. Oh, well, okay, it's actually a spiked club. And there's a ball, of course. Well, actually, a human head. But anyway, that's neither here nor there nor in your underwear. The point is that if I'm understanding this correctly, what it seems like is that you maybe could take advantage of my—how do you say—skills in the arts of reconnaissance?"

"You are going to have to tell us—in English—what exactly you are talking about," Mike said.

"I mean if they are spying on Hunter, the only proper response is to spy back," he said. "We need to go over there and see what we can find."

"If you remember correctly," I said, "I already tried that and it resulted in a little thing called ME GETTING PUNCHED IN THE FACE." I pointed to my eye. It was only a little red now, but I liked to show it off still.

"Yeah," Other Mike said, rolling his eyes. "I think you mentioned it once or twice."

I guess I had mentioned it about a thousand times. I never had a black eye before! I wanted sympathy. And people to think I was cool. It *was* cool. Traumatic and painful and I don't recommend it. But still.

"You're not worried?" I asked. "You'd have to climb up that billboard to see what you can find."

"So?" he asked.

"So?" Mike yelled. "You're terrified of heights. We've been trying to get you to go off the high dive at the pool for, like, our whole lives. You can't even stand walking on the curb and it's, like, six inches high."

"Well, I don't see any reason to tempt fate when there's a perfectly solid road right there next to the curb," Other Mike said.

"Yeah, but you're willing to climb a billboard ladder that's, like, thirty feet high?" I asked.

"Sure." Other Mike shrugged. "I mean, I'm not crazy about the idea. But if it needs to be done, it needs to be done. Anything for the team."

"This is really weird," Mike said. "You're afraid to go to the 7-Eleven down the street because you think the old guy who works there is going to beat you up."

"Well, to be fair, that old guy is really mean. Do you see the way he looks at us?"

"Other Mike," I said, "that guy is about nine hundred years old. I'm surprised he can see anything at all. I don't think he's trying to look angry, I just think he's trying to *look*. He squints like that when he's reading the paper. Plus, how tough can a nine-hundred-year-old man be?"

"Um, remember last summer when you said the same thing about Blaze O'Farrell? And he turned out to be a murderer. Plus, the guy at the 7-Eleven looks pretty wiry."

"Which brings me to my point," I said. "You're afraid of that old guy but not the possibility of someone beating you up for sneaking around Griffith's field?"

"They're stealing our secrets," he said. "I say we steal theirs. You know what they say—fight fire with fire."

"Huh," I said. "I always thought the saying was 'Fight fire with wire.'" What? I did. The Mikes laughed.

"'Fight fire with wire'? That doesn't make any sense," Mike said.

"Sure it does," I explained. "You know, you build a wire fence around the fire. It's a good way to contain the fire and keep it from spreading."

"No, that wouldn't work," Other Mike said. "Fire would just, like, go right through a wire fence. I'm quite sure it's 'Fight fire with fire.'"

"That makes no sense at all. How would you fight a fire with more fire? Wouldn't that just make the fire spread? Wouldn't it just get bigger? What are you going to do, burn a fire? Good luck with that." I was really sure of myself.

"I think it's only an expression," Mike said. "You know, like when it's raining cats and dogs, you don't literally see cats and dogs falling from the sky."

"Well, it's stupid," I said. "It should be 'Fight fire with water.' It doesn't rhyme, but it makes a heck of a lot more sense."

"Yeah, sounds great," Mike said. "Put it on a T-shirt. FIGHT FIRE WITH WATER. Can we get back to the point? How is Other Mike not afraid to go climb that billboard for us?"

"Eh," Other Mike said. "Their team will be at Highland for that game today, right? Come on, Lenny, let's go over there."

"Me?" I said. "I, um, I have . . . homework?"

It was a terrible excuse. But fine, maybe I just didn't want to get punched in the face again. If Other Mike was suddenly feeling reckless and brave, and he wasn't going to listen to reason, that was his own problem.

"I have practice," Mike said.

"So I'll have to do my secret undercover mission to Griffith's field alone?"

"You'd do that for us?" Mike asked.

"Undercover?" I asked. "I'm not sure there's a need for a disguise."

Other Mike wiggled his eyebrows. "Never go disguise-free when you can wear a disguise," he said. He was quite often trying to get us to go on spy missions. I guess our adventure last summer gave him a taste of it and he liked it. Also, for Christmas he got an amazing espionage kit. It wasn't just dumb fake mustaches and silly spy stuff; it was, like, remote-control cameras and sweet gear like that. Pretty awesome. What did I get for the holidays? Oh, right, the feeling of pure joy that comes from letting some other kid play a video game I WASN'T EVEN DONE WITH. I was impressed.

"Sure, sure," I said. "Disguise the limit."

CHAPTER TWENTY-NINE

It couldn't have been easy. It had to be nearly impossible. But he did it. Mike went up to Davis in the cafeteria. He swallowed his pride and put his own dreams of stardom aside. He did it because it would help the team. He did it because it was *right*. I went with him for moral support and/or to prevent Davis from punching Mike in the face if possible. I wasn't sure how I would do that. Maybe by creating a distraction or screaming for Mr. Donovan to come help. Of course, Donovan moved slower than a turtle with arthritis. Davis could have us both pummeled into a pulp before Donovan was even halfway across the cafeteria.

Mike walked up to Davis and tapped him on the shoulder. Davis was sitting at a cafeteria table, engrossed in lunch. *Engrossed* is the right word because he was pretty gross to watch eat. He turned around and snarled, mustard stains all over his face and everything.

"What do you want? I'm buying a fleet here," he said, or at least I thought that's what he said. It was hard to understand him because of all the food in and around his mouth.

"You get to the point, Davis," I said. "That's what I like about you."

Davis stopped chewing and stared.

"Well," Mike said. "I have—well, Lenny has—well, me and Lenny have—well, we have some news."

"Gonna get matching tattoos that say DORK and BUCKET across your foreheads? Good thinking. I can recommend a guy."

"Ha. Well, no, actually . . . Why don't you tell it, Lenny?" Mike said.

"Well," I began. "As you know, I'm a bit of a detective."

"Sure, sure," Davis said. "The case of the disappearing dork-buckets. I read all about it in *Dork-Bucket Weekly*."

"Seriously, Davis," I said. "Just zip it. We're trying to tell you something important. Something that can get you back on the team."

Davis stopped chewing. Even more remarkably,

he stopped talking. A full five seconds passed without him saying "dork-bucket." It was truly a modern miracle.

"Why would you want to do that?" he said to Mike. "I'd take your spot in a heartbeat. The only reason you're the starting catcher is that I got booted. You know that. You know I'm better."

Mike took a deep breath. Then another deep breath. This was not easy for him. Why did Davis have to make it so much harder?

"Yes," Mike said. "You are a very good catcher and you can help this team win. That's part of why I'm telling you this. Coach Zo always says that there is no *I* in *team*."

"Yeah, but there *is* a *me* in *team*," I said. "You know, if you pull out the *m* from the end and the *e* from the beginning and, like, rearrange them."

They both looked at me and rolled their eyes. See? I'm bringing people together. I'm so helpful.

Mike continued. "Davis, we know you were framed in the theft of the phone. Kyle took his own dad's phone and panicked. He didn't want his dad to know, so he stashed it in your shin guard. He let you take the fall."

"I'll kill him!" Davis said, pounding his massive fist on the table. His milk carton leapt up into the

air like the laws of gravity suddenly no longer ap-
plied.

"Well," I said. "He didn't mean it. He wasn't
trying to frame you. He was just trying to stop his
parents from getting a divorce."

"Divorce does suck," Davis agreed. "Maybe I'll
just maim him."

"That's the spirit!" I said.

"So today after school, Davis, let's go have a
little meeting with Coach Zo before practice, me
and you," Mike said. "We'll set things right."

Just then Other Mike popped up from behind
us. He started speaking in a weird high-pitched
voice. Possibly a British accent. "And *I'll* go to
Griffith on a spy mission!" he said. "If those dork-
buckets are spying on us, you know we gots to spy
on them."

"Good thinking, Other Mike," Davis said seriously. "Fight fire with wire."

Mike and I smacked our foreheads and laughed.

CHAPTER THIRTY

So Mike and Davis were competing for a starting job. Other Mike was on a spy mission. I was at home, just hanging out and thinking about my next case. Flipping through *The Semilegal Guide to Cheating at Baseball*.

Then my phone buzzed. It was a text from Mike with an update on the little prepractice meeting with him, Davis, and Coach Zo.

> MIKE: Kyle confessed. Zo sent him packing. Davis is back on the team.
>
> ME: Sorry.
>
> MIKE: Nah, it's cool. Anything to make the team better. Plus, for the first time ever, Davis is being really nice to me.

ME: I'd still keep my milk
covered.

MIKE: Oh, and I told Coach Zo
you were the one who figured
it out. He was impressed. Said
you were a great detective. A
real Hercule Poirot. However
you spell that.

I was flattered. Coach Zo knew a lot about
baseball and the detective game. He was always
reading those mystery novels.

ME: Tell him I work cheap if
he wants to figure out who is
stealing your signs.

MIKE: You're already working
on that.

ME: Yeah, and I also don't
work cheap.

MIKE: Ha-ha. Gotta run.
Practice starting.

Then the doorbell rang. It was Other Mike.
"What did you find?" I said excitedly. "Any clues?
Please tell me you didn't get beat up. Run into any

ninjas? You look fine, but you can never be quite sure with a ninja attack."

He stood there quietly. "Lenny, there's, um, a, well, a weird thing I can't of want to say but—"

"The only weird thing here is you, Other Mike. 'I can't of want to say'? That doesn't even make any sense. Just spit it out. It's not like you to be at a loss for words."

"Yeah, but this is just, you know." He started nudging me and winking. At least I think that's what he was doing. He was always twitching all over. Made it hard to read his body language.

"What on earth are you talking about?"

"I can't believe you're keeping this up."

"Keeping what up?"

"The act, Len. Come on. It's really quite impressive. I've never known you to be much of an actor. Remember when they gave you the part of the tree in, well, every school play ever?"

"I'm a perfectly fine actor! Trees play to my strengths. I'm a believable Spruce. Of course, I can also go Pine, if need be, and even on occasion if I feel like stretching it out, do a credible Oak." I paused. "Why are we talking about me being an actor?" I asked. It really didn't make any sense.

"You know," he said, elbowing me, drawing out the words. *Yoooooou knooooooow.*

"I really have no idea what you're talking about, Other Mike," I said.

"Okay, okay," he said. "If you're going to make me spell it out for you, I will. I'm really not comfortable with this, and I don't know why you just won't admit it, but fine. When I went to far field out there—"

"It's called center field," I corrected. Sheesh.

"Really?" he said. "Because you know it's not in the center of the field, right? Center is more about where the brown hilly thing is."

"'The brown hilly thing'? Um, do you mean the pitcher's mound?"

"Sure, whatever."

"Okay, but there is no such thing as 'far field' in baseball. I assure you it's center field."

"Fine, okay, whatever. When I went out into center field, I climbed up that billboard. No small feat, you know. But I did it."

"Fenner's Automobiles!" I said. "I knew it."

"Yeah, it *is*, like, the perfect spot to hide a telescope."

"Exactly."

"And, well, I found one, as I'm sure you know."

"Yeah! I mean, I wasn't *totally* sure, but I thought there might be," I said.

Other Mike stared at me for a long, long time. I couldn't read his look. It was almost like he was mad at me, but also like he was just confused. And maybe like he felt sorry for me. Other Mike can pack a lot of look into one look. I think it's the eyebrows.

"I guess it makes sense now," he said. "I can see why you were trying to talk me out of looking. The whole thing about how high it was and how I might get beat up . . . I guess you even faked the black eye."

"Wait, what?" I said. "That black eye was totally real! What are you talking about? I wasn't trying to talk you out of anything."

"Sure, Lenny. Sure," Other Mike said. "All I know is that you are not surprised that there was a telescope in the Fenner's Automobiles billboard."

"No," I said.

"And you wouldn't be," he said.

"What do you mean?"

"What I mean," he said, "is that the telescope was clearly labeled PROPERTY OF LENNY NORBECK."

Other Mike and I stood there in my living room, as still as statues. Well, he was doing his normal Other Mike twitches, but at a reduced pace.

For him, that was like a statue. As for me, I might as well have been made out of stone. I was frozen stiff! I couldn't believe it. When I finally spoke, this is what I said:

"Dude."

"Dude," Other Mike said back.

"Dude."

"Dude."

"Say something else!" I yelled.

"What do you want me to say? I get it. You didn't like Mike being on the team. You wanted to sabotage him somehow. You set up a telescope. You stole the signs, gave them to the other team. I get it, Len. And I won't say anything. I promise. I won't call the police."

"What?" I said. "The police? It's not like it's illegal."

"Well, you guys sure made a big deal out of it. It seemed like it was worse than murder, to hear you guys talking about it."

"Well, it *is* a big deal! The play-offs are coming up. Hunter is our best pitcher. We'll have to play at least one game at Griffith. And if we don't figure this out, they will win the championships and we will lose!"

Other Mike twisted up his mouth into a look of

disbelief. Then he twisted his eyebrows into a look of disbelief. He twisted his whole face into disbelief. His arms were even twisted up.

"It's pretty weird that you're so upset about this, seeing as how you're the one who was helping Griffith."

"I HAD NOTHING TO DO WITH THIS!" I was screaming. My face was red and hot, and my voice was becoming a high-pitched wail.

"Well, it kind of has your name all over it," he said. "Literally."

We stood there for a long time staring at each other.

"What do you have to say for yourself?" he said finally.

And the truth was, I had nothing at all. "Well, it really wasn't me," I said. "Did you tell anyone?"

"No," he said. "Just my dad. And Davis. And Mike maybe."

"WHAT?" I screamed. Everyone was going to be furious at me! "Why did you tell them?"

"I wasn't sure what to do!" he said. "They all said the noble thing was to come talk to you. Oh, and Davis said he wasn't surprised and he thought it was you all along. Actually, a lot of people thought it was you. I didn't want to say anything."

"What?" I said. "Why didn't you bring the telescope with you? Where's your proof? Maybe it was you!" I was getting desperate.

"It was mounted to the sign. Like with screws and stuff. Good work. I had no idea you were so handy."

"It wasn't me! There has to be a logical explanation," I said. "Other Mike, you have to believe me." And then, sports fans, what happened next was this: I started to cry. I'm not proud of it, but it's the truth. The tears came slowly at first, then they were racing down my cheeks like a base runner sprinting for home. It suddenly struck me: this is how Mike must have felt when I thought it was *him*. How could I be such a bad friend? And how could Other Mike be such a bad friend?

"Okay," Other Mike said, taking a deep breath. "Okay, okay, okay. I believe you. You really aren't this good of an actor. Let's figure this thing out together. Do you have any clues?"

"Nothing concrete," I said. "I feel like a dog chasing his tail. Everything winds back onto itself. The only clue I have is this." I handed Other Mike the checkout slip from the library. "It shows that someone had this book out before me, but I don't know who."

"What's the other book on there?" Other Mike said. "*The Murder of Roger Ackroyd?* Someone murdered that actor?"

"You're thinking of Dan Aykroyd."

"Someone murdered Dan Aykroyd?!"

"What?" I said. "No. You're getting off track."

"Do you think that if we found out who borrowed this book, we'd know who was stealing the signs?" Other Mike asked.

"It's our best shot," I said.

"Okay, then," he said. "Let's see what we can find out about it."

He took out his phone and entered the title of the book into a search engine. At first he accidentally did type "Dan Aykroyd," so it got confusing again. Then he figured it out. He started reading. "*The Murder of Roger Ackroyd* is a controversial mystery novel by Agatha Christie starring the detective Hercule Por . . . Por . . . I don't know how to say this name."

"I believe it's Poirot," I said. "You say it like *Pwa-roh.*" Where had I heard that before?

And then, like a fly ball softly landing in a center fielder's glove, the answer to the puzzle fell into my lap.

CHAPTER THIRTY-ONE

I decided to wait until the next game against Griffith to reveal what I knew. I didn't have to wait very long because of the whole three-team-league thing. It was two weeks later. Probably like in the old days of baseball when there were just two teams. The Reds and the Red Stockings. Like, "Oh, who do we play today? The Red Stockings? And tomorrow? The Red Stockings? And the day after that? Red Stockings? Got it. Perchance I shall sport my blue pantaloons. Look at my fancy mustache."

Hunter was scheduled to pitch. It was clear that someone was stealing his signs. Without cheating like a bunch of cheating cheaters, Griffith couldn't hit him. Schwenkfelder was one game up on Griffith going into the final game of the year. There was just one game left: Griffith versus

Schwenkfelder. If we won, we would clinch the championship. If we lost, the season would end in a tie. A tie, the old sports saying goes, is like kissing your sister. I don't have a sister, but it doesn't sound very good.

There was something else on my mind, though. I was doing my duties as the announcer. I pressed Play to start the national anthem. I dutifully announced the starting lineups. The umpire yelled, "Play ball." And then I made a subdued announcement. I had been doing some thinking. Deep thinking.

"Hello, ladies and gentlemen," I said. "This is your PA announcer, Lenny Norbeck. You're probably wondering why I gathered you all here today." Hey, it seemed like my only chance to say it. I realized that no one was wondering. Also that I hadn't technically gathered them. They were just there for a baseball game.

I waited for some applause. There was no applause. I continued anyway. "Well, sports fans," I said, "I need to get something off my chest. I need to get the truth out there. Sometimes the truth hurts, but it's still the truth." Again I waited for applause. There was none. Coach Zo started his way toward me, so I began to speak quickly. "The batters for the Griffith Griffins are cheating! They know the secret signs. They know what pitch is coming before it arrives. The twins are taking turns sneaking out to center field. They know the signs, so they call the coach—their father—and he flashes a sign to the batter!" I paused. Everyone's eyes were on me. It was pretty fun. I sure hoped I was right. "I should add that the person who cracked the code is not me. I don't know what you've heard, but I did not do it! Even if my name was on the telescope. Not sure what was going on there. But you are correct to look to the Schwenkfelder side to find the culprit," I continued. "You should look to Coach Zo."

Coach Zo stormed into the announcer's booth. His face was bright red and the veins on his massive arms were popping up. He looked like he might rip my head off.

"Lenny," he said through gritted teeth. "Would you shut up?"

"Are you saying it isn't true?" I said. "*You* had the book from the library. *You* had the discussion with the Griffith coach before the game. *You* murdered Dan Aykroyd!" I got kind of carried away.

"I'm just— Turn the microphone off!" he said. The microphone squealed a blast of feedback.

"Only if you tell everyone that it wasn't me!" I handed him the microphone.

"People thought it was *you* who stole the signs?" He seemed genuinely confused.

"Yes," I said. "And it wasn't. It was you. Even though my name was on the telescope!"

Coach sighed. "It was me. The signs. No idea who murdered Dan Aykroyd. Didn't even know he was dead."

I turned off the microphone. I felt so proud. Again, I expected a round of applause. There wasn't one. Most everyone in attendance was just confused. I guess it was not what they expected from a middle school baseball game.

Coach Zo spoke quietly. "I wasn't trying to frame you, Lenny," he said. "I just needed a telescope. I bought that one used at that Salvation Army store downtown."

"Discardia!" I said through gritted teeth. Still ruining my life. That must have been where Mom donated my stuff. Just a coincidence. Not a massive conspiracy to frame Lenny Norbeck.

Which meant that I just outed Coach Zo's secret plan for nothing. Oops.

Luckily, he took it well. I mean, he didn't murder me, so that was a good starting point. Hunter, on the other hand? Hunter did not take it well. He stood there on the mound with a look of total disbelief. He started screaming at Coach!

"Is this correct?" he yelled. "Is this how you treat the Great Imperial Ashwell? Is this how you treat the most amazing pitcher the game has ever known?"

"That's it," Coach hollered back. He left the announcer's booth and walked onto the field. He was yelling and everyone in the crowd was listening with rapt attention. "I guess you learned nothing! That's it! You're sitting today. Hrab, you get in there."

Henry Hrab quickly grabbed his glove and ran onto the field.

"You can't bench the Great Imperial Ashwell!" Hunter yelled.

"Oh yes, I can," Coach said.

"No, you can't," Hunter said. "Because the Great Imperial Ashwell quits."

He dropped his glove on the mound and slowly walked off the field, never looking back. Everyone was stunned. No one knew what to do for a second. The crowd became restless.

"Um, should I still get in there?" Henry said.

"Yes," Coach said. "Let's play some ball."

I turned the microphone back on and repeated his words. "Play ball!"

The game started and, long story short, we got our butts handed to us. Henry kind of got shelled. He wasn't prepared, wasn't expecting it, and, let's face it, wasn't Hunter Ashwell. So the season ended in a tie. Total sister kiss. That is, if kissing your sister is the worst feeling in the world. At least for me. Because it was all my fault! If Hunter had stayed in there, we could have won. We *would* have won. They didn't have a telescope in our park, did they? Why couldn't I keep my mouth shut?

CHAPTER THIRTY-TWO

The next few days at school, everyone was talking about what happened at the baseball game. I mean, it *was* big news. A coach stealing signs from his own team? Kind of a crazy story. Kind of a big deal.

Still, what was Coach Zo thinking? Well, I'll just let you read the interview they did with Coach Zo in the *Schwenkfelder Intelligencer*. (Our newspaper has a weird name.)

Q: So, Coach Zo, you decided to steal the signs from your own catcher and tip off the opposing team. My first question will seem like an obvious one. Why?

A: I've said it a lot of times and I'll say it again. It's my job to win baseball games, yeah, but I like to think that what I'm doing out there is a little more than that. I'm turning these young boys into men. I teach them a lot of positive traits. I teach them to work hard. I teach them to be respectful. And yes, I teach them humility.

Q: By cheating against your own team?

A: It's not cheating. Not really. If you can find something in the rulebook, I'd love to see it. And, yeah, I know it was not exactly a typical move, but it needed to be done. I tried talking to Hunter Ashwell, benching him—I tried everything. It didn't work. But Hunter needed a lesson in humility. He needed to learn what it was like to come back to earth. He needed to know that no matter how great you are, there's always someone better. And so I taught him that lesson.

Maybe I cost my team a ball game or two, but that boy won something bigger. He learned what it's like to lose. Important lesson.

And besides, there's only three teams in the league. We're still tied for first.

Q: Didn't you cost him a chance to be his best in front of a big-time scout? You might have hurt his career. His parents could sue you.

A: Oh, let them sue. And by the way, there were no scouts coming to that game. I know there was a rumor that Truck Durkin was hiding in the bushes to watch Hunter pitch. How do you think that rumor got started? *I* started it. I wanted to see how Hunter would handle the pressure. Sometimes coaches do things like that. And you know what? He handled it terribly. Grabbing the microphone before the game and giving that speech. Unbelievable.

He needed to have his world upended. It was good for him.

Q: And what do you have to say to Lenny Norbeck, your own team's announcer, who figured out that it was you who was stealing the signs from your own team?

A: Ha! Lenny's a good kid. Am I saying I wish he would have gone about sharing his discovery a different way? Sure, sure. But I'm kind of proud of him, really. Smart boy. He could have a bright future as a baseball coach if his whole career as an announcer/detective doesn't pan out.

I was famous!

It was hard to believe that it was our coach. Our own coach. The legendary Coach Zo—the man with the best winning percentage in school history. He helped us *lose* a game. *He* was the one giving signs to the other side.

On Friday I sat with Mike and Other Mike and Davis at the lunch table. We went over the events again and again.

"Can you believe it?" Davis said.

"I can't believe it," Mike said.

"I also can't believe it," Other Mike said.

As you can tell, we could not believe it.

"Coach Zo, who would have guessed?" I said. "Oh yeah, me! I'm a smart boy!" I was gloating a little.

Then Hunter walked by, carrying his lunch tray. "I don't even want to hear that name," he hissed at me.

"Come on, Hunter," Davis said. "You have to forgive him."

"Yeah," Mike said. "And you have to think twice about quitting the team."

"No, I don't," Hunter said. "I don't even need to think once about it. I'm glad I quit that stupid team. The Great Imperial Ashwell will never again pitch for that Coach What's His Name."

"Coach Zo," Other Mike said helpfully.

"I said he should not be named!" Hunter said.

"Sorry."

"Come on, man," Davis said. "We could really use you in the play-offs."

"There is no chance on earth," Hunter said. "I don't even want Schwenkfelder to win. I'm going to be cheering for Griffith to crush you."

"No way," Mike said. "That's not cool."

"And you know what?" Hunter said. "Next year, I'm going to make *sure* Griffith wins."

"What do you mean by that?" I asked.

"You'll see," Hunter said. "You'll see. Oh, you'll see, all right. Yeah, you'll see."

"I guess we'll see, then," Other Mike said.

With that, Hunter walked away.

"Well, that was weird," Mike said.

"We can still beat Griffith in a one-game play-off," Davis said.

Because the silver lining to my costing us the chance to clinch first place was that we still finished the regular season tied for first place. This is fairly common in a league with three teams. We split our games against Griffith. Both Schwenkfelder and Griffith swept Highland. That left two teams tied for first. Since there were only three teams in the league, the play-offs were just two rounds, with one team getting a bye. Since there was so often a tie, the ingenious method of a coin toss was developed to see who got to skip the first round.

As the Fates would have it, the Schwenkfelder Mustangs won that coin toss! We did it! We made it to the finals! Not that exciting really, considering it was just a coin toss. And also considering that Highland made it to the *semi*finals having lost every single game. And also considering that playing Highland was pretty much the same as getting a bye. Okay, they weren't that bad, but I knew Griffith would beat them. Which meant we would in all likelihood face Griffith in the finals.

"I know we can beat them," Davis said. "Even without the Great Imperial Dork-Bucket or our coach."

"I can't believe they're suspending Coach Zo for the rest of the season," Mike said. "He was right—he didn't technically break any rules. There's nothing in the rulebook against giving signs to the other team."

"Looks pretty bad, though," I said. "Plus, his shenanigans got me punched in the eye."

"Yeah," Davis said. "You mentioned . . ."

"So Zo is really out the rest of the way?" Other Mike said.

"Yup," Davis said.

"So who will coach the games, then? Coach Moyer?" Other Mike asked.

"Probably," Mike said. "It won't be the same without Zo, but we can still win this thing."

"Yeah, we can," Davis said. They high-fived.

Then Other Mike raised an interesting point. "Well, if Moyer becomes the head coach, who will be the assistant?"

"Good question," Mike said. "I guess we'll go with just one coach?"

"Or," Other Mike said, "you could add a student-coach."

"Is that, like, a thing?" Davis asked.

"Are you volunteering someone?" I asked. "Because I already have a job as announcer. Flattering and all. Really nice of you to suggest. I do have some thoughts about defensive shifts and bullpen management, but—"

"No," Other Mike said. "I was volunteering myself."

"Yeah?" Davis said. "You'd be great!"

"I thought you meant me," I said, kind of sad. I mean, I liked announcing, but being a coach would be more fun. Plus, did Other Mike really know anything about baseball?

"Oh, I think I have a plan for you, Lenny," Mike said.

"What?" I said.

"It's a surprise," he said.

"I hate surprises," I said.

"Too bad," Mike said. "This is a good one."

"Here's one question I still have," Other Mike said. "Why were those kids attacking Lenny for snooping around the billboard at Griffith?"

"Well, just because they weren't the ones who put the telescope there doesn't mean they weren't in on it," Mike said. "Coach Zo had to have an accomplice. He had to give the signs up to somebody. They had to have someone up in the scoreboard sending signals." He turned to me. "They saw a guy snooping around and wanted to scare you off. They probably even recognized you as a Schwenkfeldian."

"They *had* to be from the Griffith team," I said, touching my eye. It had healed, but the memory remained. "Those jerks."

"And the way to get back at them," Mike said, "is to do it on the field."

"Yeah," I said. "Beat them good for me."

Mike and Davis exchanged a look. "Why don't you beat them yourself?" Davis said.

"What do you mean?" I said, chewing on some cheese curls.

"Lenny," Mike said. "Fine—that's the surprise. I told Coach Moyer about your arm."

I stopped chewing. "What about it?" I said. I examined my arm. It just looked like an arm.

"All that time practicing throwing those wild pitches—you got really good."

"Yeah, really good at throwing wild pitches," I said.

"No, just really good at throwing. It's pretty unusual, but we could use an extra pitcher now that Hunter quit. Maybe you can make the roster for the play-offs."

I almost choked on my cheese curls. Could I really do it?! "I think you can make it through the grueling one-game play-offs without me." No one laughed. I thought we were just joking around. But they were being serious. They were being serious about me replacing Hunter Ashwell? The best pitcher in the league? The guy who threw a perfect game?

"Yeah," Davis said. "And you obviously know baseball. Plus, you're tough. And not afraid of anything."

I had no idea *who* they were talking about, but I decided just to roll with it.

Davis continued. "Being wild is not bad sometimes. Scares the hitters off. And next year I'll be in high school. You guys will have to carry this team. With Mike as your catcher here, you never have to worry about a wild pitch. I'll switch out to first base when they bring you in to pitch."

"He *is* like a Bench," Other Mike said. We laughed.

"Wait, do you mean it?" I said. "You really think Moyer will let me join the team? To pitch for the play-offs?"

"Yeah," Davis and Mike both said at the same time.

"Unbelievable! I'm going to get to pitch? Will I be a starter or a reliever? Should we go over signs? Do you think I'll get a nickname? Should I be 'Wild Thing' or maybe 'the Fireman'? How about 'the Heartbreak Kid' because of, you know, how my parents are cardiologists? Oh man, what number will I get to wear, and should I use eye black or go eye-black-free?" I asked.

"Um, maybe slow down a little," Davis said. "Have the tryout first."

I could not slow down. My mind was racing. "I'll take anything, but I have to have a nickname. 'Firpo'? 'Salty'? 'Heinie' Manush? Those are real baseball names. Never mind. How about 'Wild Bill'? Wild Bill Donovan was a good pitcher."

"Your name is not Bill," Other Mike pointed out unhelpfully.

"How about Boots Poffenberger?" I said.

"Now you're just making stuff up," Mike said. I wasn't. That's totally a real baseball player. You can look it up.

"The Lunatic?" I suggested.

"Getting warmer," Davis said. "Getting much warmer."

CHAPTER THIRTY-THREE

So after school that day, I was to join the team for practice. Me! It was the team's last practice before the big game, which was scheduled for Saturday. They had a lot to go over, what with their new coach. For indeed, Coach Moyer ascended from assistant to head coach. The assistant coach spot was vacant. Could it really be Other Mike? They had signs to go over and strategy to consider. But before that, there was the matter of filling the open roster spot vacated by Hunter Ashwell.

Coach Moyer instructed the rest of the team to warm up in the outfield while Mike strapped on the catcher's gear and Lenny "the Lunatic" Norbeck climbed the pitcher's mound. But I knew the guys weren't going to take their warm-ups very seriously. They were going to have at least one eye on the mound.

"Okay, kid," Coach Moyer said. "Newts said you got a pretty good arm, so let's see what you can do."

He tossed me the ball, and through some small miracle, I caught it. My hand was so sweaty that it was hard to grip the ball. I tried to pretend that I wasn't about to try out for the team. I tried to pretend I was just out in Mike's backyard, flinging practice tosses to him. If he believed in me, I could believe in myself.

I went into my windup and fired one hard and fast, right down the middle of the plate. It smacked Mike's mitt with a satisfying thud. I considered yelling something about how I was the Great Imperial Lenny! But it didn't seem like the right time for a joke. I just nodded like it was something I had done a million times. Which, if you thought about it, I had. All those hours practicing with Mike were paying off. But my next pitch wasn't so good, and Mike had to dive to his left to catch it. And my next one hit a pickup truck in the parking lot. But the next few were right down the middle (more or less), and Coach Moyer had seen enough. My heart was pounding.

"Well, beggars can't be choosers," he said. Man, talk about a ringing endorsement.

"Does that mean I'm on the team?" I asked.

"You got it, kid," he said. "I like a little wildness in my relievers. Keeps the batters guessing. You're just lucky that wasn't my truck. It belongs to Donovan and I hate that guy."

Again, not the most enthusiastic endorsement. But still! I was on the team! It was just for one game and it was just because Hunter had quit and it was pretty likely that I was never going to get in. But still! Lenny "the Lunatic" Norbeck, wearing a uniform. Putting on a glove. Smearing on the eye black. (I definitely needed eye black.) Lacing up the cleats. (I would need to buy cleats! My feet have grown about twelve sizes since the last time I played.) And heading to the ballpark.

"Thanks, Coach," I said. "You won't regret it." I looked over to the bleachers where Other Mike was sitting, cheering me on. "Oh, and if you happen to need an assistant coach for the big game, I know just the guy. My friend over there is an absolute genius and—"

"Does he have a pulse and the ability to carry a bucket of balls?" Coach Moyer asked.

"Um, one out of two?" I said.

"Tell him he's hired," Coach Moyer said.

Team Lenny and the Mikes.

Play ball.

CHAPTER THIRTY-FOUR

Griffith beat Highland in the first round of the play-offs, just as we knew they would. It wasn't even close. They pounded them, and before you could say "round one," the run rule went into effect. A total whooping. So this set up a one-game, winner-take-all championship game. Schwenkfelder versus Griffith. Good versus evil. Mustangs versus Griffins. Which totally isn't fair if you think about it. Griffins are half eagle and half lion. In other words, the coolest animal ever. Mustangs are just horses. And not even big ones. But anyway, in this case, the Mustangs were sure to win. If I didn't blow it! My first game would be for the trophy. I was trying to not freak out.

I was failing.

I was freaking out pretty much around ·the clock. I didn't sleep at all. I developed these big pouches under my eyes that made it look like my face was packing for a long trip. Because of the bags, I mean. Never mind. It got worse on the night before the game. I had weird dreams. All the normal nervous dreams everybody has. Like I was trying to run in wet grass but kept falling down. Like I was falling and couldn't stop. Like all my teeth were falling out into my baseball glove. Okay, that one might not be one that everyone has.

On the day of the game I woke up with butterflies in my stomach. I think the butterflies even had butterflies. And those butterflies had butterflies in their stomachs. Basically what we're talking about here is an infinite loop of butterflies in stomachs in butterfly stomachs. Nervous.

We had one game to win it all. We could have used Hunter, but still, we had Byron Lucas, who was going to start. And there was Noah Stewart, who had developed into a solid reliever. Plus, there was Henry Hrab and at least one or two other guys they could throw in there if they needed an extra arm. They could bring Mike in to pitch even if his arm would fall off. An armless Mike would probably be better than me. *Wait, no, stop it, Lenny!* (This is me talking to myself, a device I learned from a video online called *How to Psych Yourself*

Up to the Max. Part of the video was this guy putting his thumb through a block of wood. So I knew he knew what he was talking about.) I was supposed to shout down the negative thoughts with positive ones. The old Lenny would joke about how a one-armed man was a better pitcher than he was. Or a no-armed man. But the new Lenny believed in himself.

Or at least he tried.

The game was scheduled on a Saturday afternoon at our home stadium. That way all our friends and family could come. I showed up early at the park and tried to play it cool. Then I warmed up. It was confusing, trying to warm up and play it cool. I might have been overthinking it.

I watched the crowd start to arrive. The Norbecks were certainly there, looking happy and maybe a little nervous. I was feeling nervous myself. But also happy that they were there, you know? All the stuff with Kyle made me think how lucky I was, even if they were major dork-buckets. (Sorry, I've been hanging out with Davis too much.) Plus, I had to admit, Dad's advice to confront Mike really was the right thing to do. It didn't seem like it at the time, but it definitely was.

I saw Maria Bonzer was there, sitting on the

Schwenkfelder side. My side. I tipped my cap to her as I walked across the field, getting ready for the game. It felt cool, tipping my cap like that.

She waved me over. I wasn't sure if you were allowed to talk to the crowd during practice. But I was pretty sure I'd seen players in the major leagues do it.

"What's up?" I said.

"You'll never guess what I heard in the halls of Griffith Middle School yesterday," she said.

"What?" I asked.

"Swedish?"

"Huh?" I said.

"Swedish."

"Well, that explains everything."

"Don't you remember when you said that you thought the ninjas who punched you were speaking Swedish?" she said.

"Oh yeah!"

"Well, it's not actually Swedish. It's a made-up language."

"No, I'm pretty sure Swedish is a real language—"

"Shut up! I mean, I'm pretty sure what you heard wasn't Swedish but a made-up language that the Fenner twins have! I heard them talking and I asked some people about it in school. They've apparently been doing it their whole lives. Some freaky twin thing, I guess."

"Those jerks!" I said.

"Yeah," she said. "If you want to beat them up, I'm available."

"Thanks," I said. "But I think I'll beat them on the field."

It felt pretty cool saying that. I scanned the crowd and saw more familiar faces. My old babysitter—I mean *house sitter*—Courtney DeLuca even made the trip in to watch the big game. I had no idea how she knew about the game. Then I remembered that she was the daughter of one of Dad's work friends. Dad must have been talking about it at work! He was probably telling everyone he knew about how his son solved a couple of crimes and then got a spot on the team. Knowing he was actually proud of me (a rare feeling) made the butterflies acquire more butterflies.

Finally, it was just about game time. The team was all sitting in the dugout, getting psyched up to the max. I still couldn't believe I was there. At times I'd look down and see the uniform on my chest and have an out-of-body experience. It was like—*I know this is my head, but whose body is it at-*

tached to? A baseball player's? Why? How did this happen?

Then a familiar face appeared in the dugout. It was Kyle Webb.

"Pardon me, Coach," he said. "I know I'm off the team and I don't deserve to be here. But I just wanted to wish the guys good luck. And maybe fill in for Lenny as the announcer."

"Sounds great, Kyle," Coach Moyer said. "Lenny, show him the ropes."

"Don't I need to be here for the pregame meeting?" I asked. "Go over strategy?"

"Here's our strategy," he said. "Throw strikes. Catch the ball. Hit the ball. Score some runs. If possible, more runs than the other team." He shrugged and added, "That's the game called baseball." I was beginning to see why Moyer never made head coach. I was also beginning to worry, what with this genius at the helm and Other Mike in the assistant's role. But I did as I was told.

I walked with Kyle over toward the announcer's booth. "Listen," I said, "I really have to apologize for getting you into trouble like that."

"You didn't," he said. "I mean, yeah, you did. But don't be sorry. It was my own fault. I had a stupid plan and it went bad and I let someone else get

· 261 ·

in trouble for it. It really was my own fault. I shouldn't have let Davis go down for it. I've been feeling guilty all season. I mean, yeah, I'm kind of bummed that I'm not out there. . . ." His voice faded away.

"There's always next year," I said. "Help us repeat as champions."

"Knock 'em dead out there," he said. "I mean, not literally. I heard you're a little wild on the mound."

"They don't call me 'the Lunatic' for nothing," I said. "By the way, make sure you call me that when you introduce me. You know, if I get into the game."

I showed him the rest of the setup—how to use the microphone, how to turn on the CD player for the national anthem—and then it was time to play ball.

CHAPTER THIRTY-FIVE

The game began with the visiting Griffins batting. All I could do was watch, of course, and cheer from the dugout. Byron Lucas was our starting pitcher, and he looked good. He didn't seem fazed at all by the pressure, and came out working fast. He threw hard, and he threw strikes. Davis was behind the plate and Mike was manning first base. The team looked sharp and we retired Griffith easily in the first. Three up, three down.

In the bottom of the first, Jagdish Sheth pitched just as well for the Griffins. It was a pitchers' duel, as they say. Nothing–nothing through the fifth inning. It started to look like Byron was going to throw a complete game, so I started to relax. We just needed some runs. All of us guys on the bench turned our hats inside out—the classic "rally cap." It's a superstitious baseball thing. I don't know why.

For some reason turning your hat inside out is supposed to help you get a rally and score some runs. Which is kind of dumb because if it worked, wouldn't you just wear your hat like that all the time? Forget logic. Sometimes you need a rally cap, and this was one of those times.

The first batter up in the bottom of the fifth for Schwenkfelder was Byron himself. Jagdish's first pitch hit him! Was Jagdish trying to hurt him? Was that how Griffith thought they'd win this thing? They were a bunch of cheating cheaters who cheat, as I believe I mentioned before, so I wouldn't put it past them.

Byron played it cool, though. He knew that if he charged the mound and pounded Jagdish into the ground, he'd get ejected. And he wanted to finish this game. So he just took his place at first base. The next batter was none other than Mike. He wasn't the team's strongest hitter, so Coach Moyer gave the bunt sign. It wasn't a bad move. This would get Byron to second base, where he could score on a single. You hate to give up the out, but sometimes one run is all you need.

Mike did his duty and squared around for the bunt. Jagdish's pitch was low, but Mike got the bat on it. The ball squirted out in front of home plate, giving the Griffith catcher just one play. He threw to first and Byron advanced to second. When Mike came back into the dugout, everyone gave him major high fives. Bunting a guy over always gets you major props because you're sacrificing your own chance to hit for the good of the team.

The next batter up was Nathan Gub. A single could score a run and give us the lead. Gub was a decent hitter and I liked our chances. Instead, he whiffed on three straight pitches. The Schwenkfelder bench let out a disappointed sigh. But up next was Davis Gannett. "Don't worry, guys," he said to us as he walked from the on-deck circle toward the plate. "I got this."

Davis dug in at the batter's box. Jagdish threw him a couple of slow ones outside. Then, with the count at two balls and two strikes, he heaved a fastball down the middle. And Davis crushed it. I do believe that that ball might still be traveling to this day. I am pretty sure I saw it in one of those pictures the *Curiosity* rover is sending back from Mars. It was a no-doubt-about-it home run! Byron crossed the plate first, then Davis strutted across. The score was two to nothing. We didn't score again, but all Byron had to do was to get six more outs and we were champions.

It wasn't going to be that easy.

Griffith started the top of the sixth with a rally of their own. In fact, the first three batters hit the ball hard. They were only singles, though, loading the bases. The next batter hit a perfect ground ball right up the middle for a double play. Two outs were recorded, but one run came in. That brought the bad guys within one run. The score was two to one. Byron was looking tired. Still, he needed just one out to get to the seventh and final inning. Coach Moyer conferred with Other Mike and they decided to leave him in.

Byron responded with a sweet series of fastballs to record the strikeout and end the inning. He looked pretty happy as he walked off the mound. But also pretty tired.

We couldn't get anything going in the bottom of the sixth. We were heading to the final frame with a one-run lead.

CHAPTER THIRTY-SIX

Coach Moyer, Other Mike, and Byron huddled for a discussion before the top of the seventh. From where I sat at the end of the bench, I couldn't hear a word. But it was clear: they were taking him out. He was tired. His arm was shot. The Griffins were hitting him hard and the lead was down to one run. I felt a knot in my stomach. They weren't going to bring *me* in, were they?

They were.

"All right, Len," Coach Moyer said, walking down toward the end of the bench. "My assistant here says you're the man for the job, and he's a heck of a lot smarter than I am. So you're the man for the job. Get in there and get us some outs."

I couldn't believe it. For a second I thought I was dreaming. But I still had all my teeth, so it couldn't be a dream. I was really getting into the game. In the last inning. With a one-run lead. For the championship.

I walked—more like floated—out to the mound. Mike came over and said a few words to me. I had no idea what they were. It was like I knew his mouth was moving, but I could not recognize the words. It was all *muh-muh-muh-muh-muh-muh*. I nodded, wondering what I had agreed to.

I took my warm-up pitches and they were terrible. I was announcing my own warm-ups in my head.

He has less control than a toddler in potty training. He's firing warm-up tosses like a blind monkey playing darts.

Finally I got one over the plate and it was time to start the game. I had no idea who the first batter was. He was just a green blur. My eyes could barely focus. Somehow, shockingly, this worked to my advantage. My first pitch was a ball, but the next three were fast ones right down the middle. I struck him out!

The crowd goes wild as Norbeck strikes out the first batter he faces. He's on his way to getting a win for his team. He's totally psyched up to the max.

The next batter stepped in. I had calmed down a little, which somehow did not work to my advantage. I walked him on four pitches. The next batter I did recognize. It was Robert Fenner. I thought he'd be up there being patient since I just walked a guy with four very wild ones, but he was swinging first pitch. And he laced that first pitch into left-center field. The guy from first made it all the way to third. Uh-oh. It was runners on first and third with just one out. Not an ideal situation. But a double play would get us through the inning.

Norbeck is going to try to throw some low ones here, to try to get a ground ball and a double play. Of course, if he throws it too low and it's a wild pitch, a run will score and tie the game. Good thing his personal catcher, the great backstop Mike DiNuzzio, is over there. Newts settles in, and here's the pitch. . . . The runner breaks for second! That's a stolen base. Not even a throw. Newts has had some arm troubles over the years and the Griffins take advantage of it. Now we're really in a pickle. Runners on second and third with one out. No chance for the double play.

Coach Moyer stepped out of the dugout, calling time. Was he taking me out of the game already? I gave up one walk and one single! That's it! Didn't he see that awesome strikeout? I knew I could find the plate if I had to. Then I saw Other Mike following along behind him.

"What's up?" I said. "I'm feeling good. Feeling good." It was a lie.

"I don't know if I agree," Coach Moyer said. "But my assistant here has an idea."

"Yeah," Other Mike said. He paused. "So, well, we got runners on second and third here with one out. That means that there is no force play and no chance to double them up."

I knew all this, of course, but I was shocked to hear Other Mike say it. It was like suddenly finding out that your dog was fluent in French. Usually it's just barking and licking itself and then all of a sudden it comes out with *"Bonjour, madame, je suis un chien."* Focus, Lenny!

Other Mike continued. "So I say we walk this guy. I've scouted the on-deck hitter, Trebor Fenner. He has a severe chop of a swing. He has no patience and he always hits the ball on the ground. Load the bases, pitch to Fenner, get the double-play ball, go home champions. Got it?" He slapped me on the butt, just like a big-league manager would do.

"Other Mike?" I said. "Is that you?"

"Don't look at me like I'm a French-speaking dog," he said. "You don't spend a few million hours with you dorks and not pick up some baseball. So you gonna do it or not?" By then Mike had joined our conference on the mound, walking up from behind the plate. He lifted his mask.

"What's the plan, gentlemen?" he asked. His face was sweating.

"Let's walk this guy," I said. "Load the bases. Load 'em up nice."

"You're the boss," he said.

"Hey, Coach," I yelled at Other Mike as he walked toward the bench. "If we win this thing, I owe it all to you."

Mike went back behind the plate and held out his arm to the side, giving the sign for an intentional walk. I heard a gasp from the crowd, but maybe that was just my imagination. Maybe not. Because while Other Mike's plan did make sense, there was of course a downside. With the bases loaded, there was nowhere to put Trebor. If I walked him, the tying run would score. If I hit him with a pitch, the tying run would score. If I threw a wild pitch, the tying run would score. If he got a hit, the tying run would score. There were so many ways the tying run would score! *But no, Lenny. Don't think negative thoughts. Believe in yourself. Put your thumb through that board!*

This was a dandy little pep talk I was giving myself. The only problem was that I accidentally said the last part out loud. Pretty much everyone looked at me like I was nuts. I decided to just go with it. It was all part of my persona as the Lunatic. I repeated it loudly. "Put your thumb through that board!" I hoped it would catch on. Maybe start a chant. I could hear the crowd. "Put your thumb through that board! Put your thumb through that board!" No such luck. It was quiet. Too quiet.

And it all came down to me and Trebor. Trebor Fenner. The bases were loaded, with his brother Robert on second base. Everyone on the Griffith side was yelling and cheering and screaming for Trebor. The ninjas! They were the ones who punched me in the face! I wanted to throw the ball through Trebor's stupid head. But of course I couldn't. A hit batter would force in a run and tie the game. Mike's words echoed through my head: *"The way to get back at them,"* he had said, *"is to do it on the field."*

I took a deep breath. I went into my windup. I

pitched. And it was about fifteen feet outside. Mike caught it, somehow, saving a run. He pointed his glove at me in that catcher's gesture that means "Settle down." I wasn't sure if I could. I took a deep breath and fired another one, this time right across the plate for a strike. Trebor smiled. He apparently wasn't going to swing. He was going to make me throw strikes. No problem, I thought, and threw another perfect one. Only the stupid blind ump called it a ball! Okay, maybe it was a *little* high. Still, he could have given it to me.

It didn't matter. You can't dwell on a bad call. You have to throw the next pitch. My heart felt like it was punching me in the face. That doesn't make sense, but somehow explains it. I was losing it. I took a deep breath and threw this one right down the middle. The count was two balls and two strikes. They always say that's an "even count," but it favors the pitcher. I only needed one more strike.

I wound up and fired, a high fastball. This time Trebor did swing. And he did miss. Strike three! I leapt off the mound, throwing my glove up into the air! I was waiting for my team to rush me, to hug me, to carry me off on their shoulders victorious! I *was* the Great Imperial Lenny the Lunatic,

Destroyer of Worlds! "Yeeeee-hah!" I screamed as my glove soared toward the sky. "We win!"

It was then that I realized there were only two outs. Everyone was looking at me like I was the proverbial French-speaking dog. I kind of wished I was. I wished I was anyone or anything else at that moment. How embarrassing! To celebrate the victory with just two outs! I felt like such an idiot. My glove fell back to earth with a sad plop.

"Just kidding!" I said. *Good one, Lenny.*

Even through his mask I could see that Mike was laughing.

There was one batter left. Jaxon Sadler was coming up to hit for Griffith. Stupid Jaxon. My heart started to beat faster as I realized he *would* be the last batter, for me anyway. I'd get him out and we'd go home champions. Or he'd get on base and the tying run would score. Maybe even the go-ahead run. Moyer would take me out for sure. Other Mike couldn't stop him. It was really amazing that he learned so much about baseball. But if he knew so much, why would he choose to use me in this situation? He must believe in me. Which meant I could believe in myself.

I settled in against Jaxon. The bases were still loaded. There was no room for error. You can only have one coach's conference on the mound per inning, so I couldn't ask Other Mike for the scouting report. I seemed to remember from earlier in the year that Jaxon was a free swinger. Not the kind of guy likely to take a walk. He was going to take his hacks. He was going to swing. I'd have to make sure he missed.

The first pitch was a little bit inside, and sure enough, Jaxon took a rip. He blasted the ball, but foul. It went about five hundred feet down the left-field line. "Don't worry, Lenny," I heard a voice say from the bleachers. It was my dad. "Just a long strike." Always the optimist, that guy. At least I had the count in my favor. I threw another one hard and Jaxon swung right through it. I was feeling it. The count was no balls and two strikes. One more strike could win it. I went into my windup and fired. It bounced about six feet in front of home plate. But true to form, Mike blocked it. Just a ball. One ball and two strikes. Still in my favor. The next pitch was about six feet high. Mike caught that one too. Two balls and two strikes. Time to focus in. I threw a fastball right down the middle, but Jaxon fouled that one off too. He was a pesky hitter. I kept firing good pitches and he kept fouling them off.

"Come on, Lenny." I heard Dad from the bleachers again. "You got this." I looked over at him. And had the greatest idea ever. The Vulcan change. Of course! It was the secret family pitch, passed through the generations. Never mind that I had never practiced it. It was a sign. It *had* to work. I stepped off the mound and motioned for Mike to come for a conference. The Griffith side groaned. They were tired of these conferences. I didn't care!

"What's up?" Mike said.

I put my glove over my mouth in case there were lip-readers or spies anywhere. We hadn't been using signs because I only had one pitch. But this was different. "I'm going to rear back like I'm throwing the cheese, but it'll be a slow one. The Vulcan change."

"Are you sure this is the time to try a pitch you've never done before?" Mike asked.

"It has to work," I said. "Nothing else is."

"Well, make it a good one," he said.

Mike snapped his mask back down and took his place behind the plate. All I needed was one strike to win. I slid the ball into my fingers, Vulcan-style. I went into the windup and let it rip like I was throwing the fastest fastball in the world. The ball sort of fluttered out of my hand, very slowly. And also not very accurately. It bounced way in front of the plate and took a wild hop.

Mike threw his mask off and began frantically looking around behind him. Oh no! It was a wild pitch! The ball was on its way to the backstop! The tying run was crossing the plate! The Griffith fans were going wild! Then Mike stepped in front of the plate and tagged the runner with his empty glove. Only it wasn't empty. He showed the glove to the umpire. The umpire yelled, "You're out!"

I was confused. Everyone was confused. What had just happened? "The ball was in my glove the whole time!" Mike yelled. "I pretended it got past me. Nothing gets past me! You should know better! I'm a Bench!"

"You certainly are!" I yelled. "Does this mean we won?"

"Yes!" he hollered.

"Why isn't anyone celebrating?" I asked.

"Good question. Let's celebrate!"

This time I wasn't the only one who threw my glove up in the air. Everyone did. We won! Kyle screamed into the microphone. People were swarming everywhere, running and hugging. And I mean everyone. The team, the fans, kids from school, Maria, my parents, everyone. There was lots of hugging and so much high-fiving that my palm hurt. It was kind of weird that I won the game on a wild pitch, but kind of right. That's the way the Lunatic does things.

In the chaos of people rushing everywhere, my parents found me and hugged me tight. "Oh, Lenny," my mom said. "We're so proud of you. Special treat tonight. Any present you want."

"Anything?" I asked.

"Sure," Dad said.

I thought about it for a minute. Maria Bonzer came up to give me a high five while I thought.

"You know, I don't want anything for me," I said to my parents.

"That's wonderful!" my mom said. "You have learned the true meaning of Discardia."

"Uh, no," I said. "That holiday still sucks. But I do want to *give* a gift for my special present. Maria needs a new phone. Some jerk stole hers."

"That's what you want?" Mom asked. "We're offering to buy you anything and you want to buy the librarian's niece a phone?"

"Sure," I said. "It's important."

"It is?" Maria said.

"Yep," I said. "That way you can call me some-times."

"Awwww," my mom said.

"For cases!" I said. "To work on cases! We're a detective team. And we're the best."

"Sure you are," Dad said. "Sure you are."